NEWPORT BEGINNINGS

CINDY NICHOLS

PRICKLY PEAR PRESS

ONE

The light over Newport Harbor was changing, from pink and yellow to almost dark purple and the stars began to twinkle. The warm, California breeze tickled Jen's neck, and she wanted just another moment out on the deck at the fundraiser.

When she'd arrived at her family's beach house before Memorial Day, she'd never in a million years thought it was going to be such a challenge to talk her family out of selling it. It had been a close call—they'd had buyers who'd wanted to tear it down—but she and her best friends, Faith and Carrie, had managed to convince her brother that it needed to stay in the family.

And the last few weeks had been spent putting together the lovely fundraiser for the children's wing of the local hospital that she was attending now.

In the fading light, she looked over at her friend, Joe, whom before this summer she hadn't seen in twenty years. But it was as if he'd never left, that she'd never married, been widowed and raised two boys on her own. Right now, in the soft breeze, there was only now.

It was Jen's favorite time of day, even more than sunrise. She hated to leave it, but, Joe nudged her, taking her out of her reverie.

"I think we'd better go back inside, don't you? I'm anxious to see what the bids are for my dad's Disney figurines. We worked so hard getting them together. I'm hoping that they fetch a good price for the hospital."

Jen sighed and looped her arm through his when he offered. She felt his warmth through his suit, and it was comforting. So far, the fundraiser had gone without a hitch and she, too, was interested to see what the figurines were going for.

Inside the beautifully-decorated ballroom, Jen leaned over the white linen-covered table and squinted. She reached up to grab her glasses from on top of her head but they weren't there.

"Your glasses are on the table, but I can tell you there are more digits than I imagined there would be."

Jen looked up at Joe. His dark brown eyes danced with glee as he pointed his thumb toward the figurines they'd spent days cataloguing and cleaning from his late father's Disney collection.

"I guess it was all worth it. It's truly amazing. Very generous of you and your mother to donate to the fundraiser."

Joe shrugged and shoved his hands in his pockets, but not before he gave a thumb's up to his mother. She clapped and waved back, a smile from ear to ear.

"This is what Ma wanted. And what my dad would have wanted, too. The children's wing at the hospital was a favorite charity of theirs. All is right with the world, it seems."

Jen sighed. Moments earlier, she'd watched the Labor Day sun set over the Newport Harbor, its light dancing on the rippling water, and wondered how she'd gotten so lucky. Although she'd spent the entire summer at her family's beach house, it had been mere weeks that they hadn't had to worry about it being sold from under them.

She'd barely had a chance to get over the surprise and settle in, and now here she was at a ritzy fundraiser where they'd raised millions for the children of her new home town.

New home town? Where had that thought come from? She had a house inland, where she'd raised the two boys after her husband had died suddenly, decades ago. Three months ago, it had been the only true home she'd ever known as an adult and had no intention of leaving it. But somehow over the summer, through spectacular sunrises, daily walks on the beach and sunset gatherings with family and friends, it seems that things had changed forever.

With all the commotion about the fundraiser—her friend Carrie was in charge but had enlisted Jen and Faith for donations for the silent auction—she hadn't told either of them what she'd decided.

She looked around the room again, wondering how her decision would change things. Carrie lived full time at the beach, her dental practice a fixture on the boulevard. Joe had told her only moments ago that he'd be staying in Newport and selling his accounting practice in Chicago, and that he and his mother had agreed to keep their gondola business going. But Faith would be leaving shortly, back inland to take up her teaching position, and things would change forever.

She'd tell them all tomorrow morning on their beach walk, she decided. Things were going so well with the fundraiser, she didn't want to take the focus off of Carrie and Dirk's great success.

"Things really couldn't have gone any more smoothly, it seems," Joe said.

Jen smiled up at him, having had the same thought, and he squeezed her elbow.

"Uh-oh. Maybe I spoke too soon."

Jen followed his gaze to the corner of the ballroom. Darn, where were her glasses? She had to squint to see what he was nodding toward, and it took a second for her gaze to clear.

"Oh," Jen said slowly, her heart sinking.

Joe nodded. "I haven't seen Carrie's mom in probably twenty years. She looks the same. And *they* look the same."

Jen knew exactly what Joe meant. Carrie's mom was lovely, and tonight for the fundraiser she'd asked Carrie to organize, she'd pulled out all the stops. Her black hair was pulled up into a chignon with a diamond pin placed perfectly. Her drop diamond earrings sparkled in the low chandelier light, and her sequined silver evening gown swooshed over her slender figure as she shook her head at Carrie.

"Carrie looks like she's holding her own. Just like she always has."

Jen wasn't so sure about that. Her dear, lifelong friend looked as if she was having a little difficulty holding her tongue—a skill she'd honed over a lifetime of listening to her mother complain. About anything and everything.

Carrie had become quite immune to it all, much to her credit, and usually shrugged it off pretty well. But there was something about her expression now that niggled at Jen and made her think that maybe it wasn't as easy as it usually was for her friend to let things roll off her back.

"Think we should go over and interrupt?" Joe asked, running his hands through his hair. "You know, like we did when we were kids?"

Jen grinned. "That was a little different. Back then, we were just trying to sneak out of the house to go to the Fun Zone, or cover for Carrie when she wanted to go sailing. I think the stakes might be a little higher at the moment."

"Hm, I thought the stakes were pretty high back then." Joe laughed when Jen nudged her elbow into his ribs and rolled her eyes.

They'd all been such good friends then, running around Newport like they didn't have a care in the world. And they didn't, back then. But a lot had happened between then and now.

"Carrie's mom sure is on a roll," Faith said when Jen and Joe got back to their table. Her eyes were big and her eyebrows raised as she clearly tried not to stare.

"That woman," Joe's mother, Mrs. Russo, said,

plonking her chianti on the table. "She's a piece of work, that one. Always has been."

When Joe, Carrie, Jen and Jen's late husband Allen were gallivanting across the beaches and harbor eating frozen, chocolate covered bananas and nursing their sunburns, the older generation had had their own interactions. And not all of them good.

"Isn't this just the best fundraiser ever, if I do say so myself," Dirk Crabtree said as he sat down at the table, all smiles. He picked up his cocktail and held it up to the others, and it seemed to take him a moment to notice that nobody was joining him in the gesture.

Jen pointed to the corner of the ballroom and he turned and looked over, shook his head and set down his glass. "Excuse me a moment. It appears that my fundraiser co-chair could use a bit of cavalry."

Jen watched as Dirk crossed the ballroom. "That's really nice of him. When we met him, remember thinking he was the typical Mr. Newport? Silk tie, fancy car, picture on bus benches? Maybe there's more to him than it seems."

Faith nodded. "Maybe. What do you think's going on?" Faith asked. Both Mrs. Russo and Jen shook their heads.

"No telling. It's always something, though. That poor girl," Mrs. Russo said. "Could be earth-shattering to her mom, like she doesn't like the flowers on the tables. Could be as simple as she doesn't like Carrie's dress. But from the looks of it, she's not complimenting Carrie on a job well done."

"Ingrate," Mrs. Russo said under her breath. "This fundraiser wouldn't even be happening if Carrie hadn't agreed to coordinate it for her mother."

"Ma," Joe admonished, holding a finger to his lips.

"Don't you shush me, Joey. You know I tell the truth."

"Well, can you tell the truth a little quieter?" Joe closed his eyes and pinched the bridge of his nose.

Jen laughed, grateful that other people saw Carrie's mother the way she did. Never satisfied, and constantly meddling. It was a wonder that Carrie even spoke to her at all.

Jen watched as Dirk seemed to smooth things over. Carrie even smiled at him with an unmistakable look of gratitude and relief. Dirk nodded at Mrs. Westland. He held out his arm for Carrie, who gratefully took it, and brought her back to their table.

Carrie sat down with an audible "oof", leaned her elbows on the table rested her chin in her hands.

"Care for anything from the bar?" Dirk asked.

"Yes, please. I'll have one of everything," Carrie said with a groan.

"What the heck was that about?" Faith asked.

Carrie took a deep breath. "You won't believe me if I tell you."

Mrs. Russo smiled warmly. "I hope it wasn't about your dress. I think it's beautiful. Perfect. Your mother is always dressed over the top anyway."

"Ma—"

Mrs. Russo shot a look at her son but did stop talking.

Carrie glanced down, and Jen was positive that it wasn't about the dress. Carrie looked as if she didn't even remember what dress she was wearing. No, it was something more.

"You okay?" Jen asked quietly as she scooted her chair closer to Carrie's.

"I don't know. I hope so."

"What's going on?" Jen asked, frowning. She couldn't imagine what would be worth arguing about at such a successful event. Carrie and Dirk had worked hard on this fundraiser, just as Mrs. Westland had asked, and it had turned out wonderfully.

"My mother chose until now to inform me that she'd extended a few extra invitations. Without letting us know."

Jen glanced around the room, taking in the fancy suits, tuxedos, evening gowns and diamonds. She couldn't even guess who wasn't there, as she hadn't really hob-knobbed much with this crowd. All the Newport Beach elite seemed to be here, famous and non-famous. But as she looked around and reached into her memory, her stomach tightened. It hadn't even occurred to her that one of Newport's most famous residents was missing, because of course he wouldn't be welcome here. They wouldn't be welcome here. It would be unkind to Carrie. But knowing Carrie's mother, it just might be something she'd do.

The thought was so awful, she could barely form it into words. "Don't tell me she invited Rob. And Cassidy."

Carrie looked over at Jen, and then over at the door, as a crowd started to gather and people turned in that direction. People began to twitter and crane their necks to see who had entered, and as the doors began to close, Jen spotted a familiar Maserati parked right out front, the attendants gushing over it.

Carrie closed her eyes and nodded slowly. "Yep. She did."

TWO

The pained expression on Jen's face matched how Carrie felt at the sight of her ex-husband and the bimbo he'd left her for. Granted, it had been quite a while ago and most of the shock had worn off, but she also hadn't seen him but a few times since and that had made it a little bit easier. Sort of.

The response of the crowd did rub things in a little bit. While she wasn't remotely interested in seeing him, apparently all the people at the fundraiser were. And he always did know how to make an entrance—especially since his wife, Cassidy, loved that kind of thing and was sort of a celebrity in her own right. If you could call it that.

She'd tried to ignore how famous he was as things had gotten progressively difficult and personal. She'd almost forgotten what it felt like to be on the cover of all the tabloids during that times and still made a point of not looking at them when she was in line at the grocery store.

Carrie tried not to look as the crowd buzzed, and she silently thanked Faith for continuing to keep their table in light conversation, pretending that there was no commotion. But soon, she couldn't ignore it any longer.

"Oh, no," Jen said, her eyes wide. She was doing her best not to look at the ballroom door, but she was facing that direction and really couldn't help it. "They brought Bethany."

Carrie's heart froze in her chest for a moment, and she couldn't catch her breath. Bethany? He wouldn't have done that. Couldn't have. They'd argued endlessly about dragging her to these kinds of events—Carrie thought it wasn't fair to Bethany, but Rob thought she needed to learn how to mingle. It appeared that Cassidy shared Rob's feelings about what kind of "education" Bethany needed, but Carrie's heart went out to the teenager. Carrie knew how much she hated these things.

She turned slowly in her chair and caught a glimpse of a young girl, dressed to the nines, her long, blonde hair falling around her shoulders. Her blue chiffon evening gown was beautiful—and clearly very expensive—but she was terribly thin and one strap had slipped off her shoulder. She was so pretty, as she always had been, but Carrie couldn't help but notice that she looked miserable. Especially when her step-mother gave her a look and slipped her strap back up on her shoulder.

Bethany. Carrie hadn't seen her in several years, and she was a sight for sore eyes. She'd missed her terribly.

"You okay?" Jen asked, resting her hand on Carrie's.

Carrie nodded, and they both watched as Carrie's mother rushed over to greet the three new arrivals, truly in her glory as the crowd parted for her. She shooed the crowd away and led them to a waiting table, already set with champagne flutes and a very expensive bottle of bubbly. As they walked through the room, Cassidy smiled and nodded to people, almost as if she were royalty, and Bethany trailed behind.

"What are you going to do?" Jen asked as the famous couple took their seats.

"I don't know. I'd like to wiggle my nose and be home in my sweats, honestly. Can I?"

Faith laughed. "You can try. I've been trying for years but haven't mastered it yet. Let me know if you get it."

"I guess I need a plan B, then. Could I sneak out the back door?" Carrie stole a glance over at her ex. She didn't want to, but she couldn't help herself. As much as she wanted to disappear, she had a hard time taking her eyes off of Bethany, and as she looked at the table, Bethany caught her eye.

The pain in her heart took her by surprise. She'd thought she'd buried all of that long ago, given up when Rob wouldn't let her see Bethany anymore. But now that she was here, in the room, all she wanted to do was hug her. It didn't matter one whit that when she last saw her, Bethany had been only twelve. She'd only been allowed to speak to her on the phone since then, and while she'd made a point of calling regularly in the beginning, Bethany had gotten involved in school and sports, and the calls had dwindled over the years.

Carrie's hand flew to her chest as she watched Cassidy shrug off her mink stole—mink! On Labor Day! —and shove it and her clutch toward Bethany. She thought maybe Bethany rolled her eyes before she went to take it to the cloak room, but she couldn't be sure.

Now that she was so close, Carrie wanted to talk to her—badly. To see how she was. To see why she was so miserable. To see if she could help. She'd always gotten the impression that Bethany would change things if she could, but she had no idea what she was feeling now. Judging from the look on her face, not much had changed.

"I have no interest in talking to Rob or that bimbo. I'd

love to see Bethany, though. It's been a long time. I miss her," Jen said, glancing back at the table.

"Me, too," Carrie said quietly.

"Oh, gosh, I'm sorry, Carrie. I didn't mean to...I meant to say..."

Carrie shook her head to stop Jen. They all knew what Bethany had meant to her, and they all knew how completely her heart had broken when it had become clear that Rob was not going to let her continue her relationship with her step-daughter. Jen had meant no harm.

But what was she going to do? She needed to figure out a way to talk to Bethany just for a minute without Rob or Cassidy around. And she thought maybe she had the perfect idea.

THREE

"I know you want to talk to her." Jen always did know what Carrie was thinking, almost as soon as Carrie did herself.

"I do. Trying to come up with a way to get her away from that table. She looks miserable."

"She sure does," Jen agreed with a nod. "And Rob and Cassidy are holding court, completely ignoring her. As usual."

Faith looked over toward the table right in front. "I can't believe they even have special flowers on their table. And Dom Perignon."

Carrie had noticed it, too. "You'd think as the organizers, Dirk and I would have seen that coming. My mother was pretty sneaky this time, even for her."

"Sheesh. It's just like a parade of people going by.

You'd think that they were rock stars or something. Not just your average reality TV stars."

"What are they?" Joe asked, leaning closer toward Carrie. "I left before you two got together. I thought he was a cook. At least that's how I remember him."

"He was, back in the day. And a poor one at that. Wasn't until he opened his restaurant that things changed for him. And for us." Carrie took another look at Rob, almost against her will. He was still incredibly handsome, but the way he was holding court and fawning over his bleached-blonde wife turned her stomach. He was almost unrecognizable to her—literally not the man she'd fallen head over heels with. Him and his daughter.

"When he opened The Wreck, everything went weird. And when Cassidy turned up to decorate for the restaurant, it really went to hell."

"Well, The Wreck seems like an appropriate name," Joe said with a raised eyebrow.

"I know, right? It was supposed to mean shipwreck, but it fits."

Jen sighed and turned toward Carrie. "I'm sorry."

Carrie shook her head. "It's all right. Honestly, I should have seen it coming."

Faith's updo almost came undone as she shook her head and frowned. "Nope. Nobody in their right mind would have seen that coming. Too fast. And so, so wrong."

Carrie nodded gratefully. At least her friends knew the real story, even if the whole world had been told something else entirely, right on the front page of the tabloids.

"Old news now. But I'd really like to talk to Bethany. I miss her."

"I bet," Jen said. "You were her mom for a very long time."

Carrie stiffened as Bethany got up from the table and headed toward the ladies' room. She stood and dropped the napkin she'd been twisting onto the table. "Looks like maybe now's my chance."

"Do you want someone to go with you?" Jen asked. She looked worried, and Carrie understood why, but she thought she should do this on her own.

"No, I think I'm okay. Thanks, though." Carrie made a bee-line for the restroom behind Bethany, glancing at Cassidy. The crowd surrounding their table had gotten even heavier so Carrie ducked inside, hoping it would stay that way for at least a few minutes.

She paused at the doorway and watched as Bethany stared at herself in the mirror. She opened her beaded clutch purse and pulled out some lipstick, leaning forward to the mirror as if she was going to put some on.

Glancing down at her hands, she put the cap back on the tube and dropped it in, closing the clutch without applying any.

"Looks like it would be pretty with that gorgeous dress," Carrie said softly as she stepped up behind Bethany.

Bethany spotted her first in the mirror, the look in her eyes clearing quickly.

Carrie watched as her expression changed from surprise, to confusion and then quickly to what she thought was anger.

Bethany turned quickly, the chiffon of her dress rustling against the counter.

"Oh, Carrie. Hello," Bethany said as she flipped her blonde hair back over her shoulder. "Lovely to see you."

The words echoed against the tiled walls and felt like a cold slap to Carrie. She took a step backward, although she hadn't meant to.

She took in a deep breath and gathered herself. "Nice to see you, too, Bethany. You look lovely."

Bethany glanced Carrie up and down. "Thank you. Your dress is...orange. As usual."

Carrie thought she saw a flicker of a smile on Bethany's lips but couldn't be sure.

"Yes. It's still my favorite color," she said, thinking it sounded kind of lame, even if it was true. "How are you?"

Bethany turned back to the mirror, retrieving the lipstick and this time putting some on. She glanced at Carrie in the mirror.

"I'm fine. Why wouldn't I be?"

"Um, you didn't exactly look like you were enjoying yourself out there. To me, anyway."

Bethany turned again, gripping her clutch tightly against her waist.

"Oh, we go to these kinds of things all the time. Cassidy and my dad are quite famous, you know. Everyone loves them. The TV show is a hit."

"So it seems." Carrie had watched it once, in the beginning, and it had made her so angry she'd never watched again. She had heard, though—or seen on the tabloids—that it was doing very well.

"Yes. And now that it's on hiatus, we're taking a tour of the continent."

Carrie's eyebrows rose. She hadn't heard anyone use that terminology for visiting Europe in decades. Sounded like something Cassidy would say.

"Well, that sounds very nice," Carrie said. "You'll be missing school. And tennis season. What about that?"

Before Bethany had a chance to respond, Jen's loud whistle pierced the air and bounced around the ladies' room right before she poked her head in.

She crooked her finger at Carrie. "Time to go." She

nodded at Bethany, and got a smile from the teenager in return. More than what Carrie had gotten.

"Well, nice to see you. Have fun on your trip," Carrie said as she followed Jen out the door. Jen grabbed her hand, pulling her faster and ducking into an alcove on the side. They watched as Cassidy swooshed into the ladies' room, and came out a second later with Bethany in tow.

"Never dismiss the importance of having a wing-man," Jen whispered. "I thought you might need one."

"Thanks. I guess I did."

"How'd it go?" Jen asked as they skirted the side walls and headed to their table.

"Ugh," was all Carrie could say. It had been confusing to her, Bethany's response not at all what she'd expected. But she didn't really know what she had hoped for anyway.

"Well, that doesn't sound promising."

"It wasn't," Carrie said.

She plopped back into her chair and turned to Dirk.

"Dirk, we're pretty well wrapped up here, aren't we? Clean-up crew is all set, Mother will be making fundraising announcements. Would you join her and make my excuses for me? I think I want to just get out of here."

Dirk frowned, but nodded. "I'd rather you'd stay, but

I understand. I'm sorry. It was a lovely evening, and a success to be proud of."

He stood as Carrie gathered up her things, buttoning his tux and heading for Carrie's mom.

Feel free to stay if you want," she said to Faith and Jen. "And thanks for coming, Mrs. Russo, Joe. Mrs. Grover, nice to see you again."

She straightened her shoulders, set her eyes on the door and walked straight out of the building. It wasn't until the valet brought her car that she realized Faith and Jen were right behind her, as always.

"Thanks, guys. I just couldn't stay."

Faith squeezed her elbow. "And we wouldn't stay without you."

"No. You did a great job, but we'll have more fun on the deck. Just the three of us," Jen said. "The past can stay in the past."

FOUR

Jen poured the last of the chardonnay into Faith's glass and glanced at her lifelong friend as they both watched Carrie head down the stairs to her car. The orange satin fabric of her formal gown that had gleamed earlier in the evening was now crumpled and dull. But there was the familiar spring in her step that never seemed to fade.

No matter what life threw at her, Carrie was always a "glass half full" kind of person, but Jen wouldn't have blamed her if she saw things differently after what had happened at the fundraiser.

She'd tried to bring it up, thinking Carrie might want to talk about it. But she hadn't. She'd just said it was nice to be able to see Bethany, that she was so grown up. Jen had even cast the bait that her mom had behaved horribly, but Carrie hadn't taken it. She'd seemed a little sad, but stoic as usual. And she hadn't stayed long, saying she needed to get out of her evening gown or she was going to lose her mind.

It certainly wasn't how Jen would have reacted. "Between her mom being such a jerk and running into Bethany—and Rob and Cassidy—I'd be furious, if it was me. I think we should have poked them all in the eye. Or spilled something on them. Accidentally, of course."

Faith, who'd known Carrie almost as long Jen had, shook her head. "Not what Carrie wanted. In the last thirty years, I've seen Carrie flustered maybe twice. If that. And even then, she bounced back pretty fast."

Jen nodded slowly. "I know. But those couple of times were like body slams. Rob skipping out with Cassidy in the dark of night, leaving Bethany with Carrie until it suited him to take her away for good? I haven't even seen him since—what, four years now?"

"Neither have I," Faith mused. "Except on TV."

"Oh, right. There's that."

"Who'd want to have that in their face? *Wives of Newport Beach* is as ridiculous as it is horrible."

"I never watched it ever again after that time you and I did. Just seeing them at the restaurant Rob and Carrie had worked so hard on was disgusting. Remember?"

"I'll never forget. It was gross," Faith said.

"At least she had her practice to fall back into.

Losing a child you'd raised from a baby overnight—I can't even imagine."

Faith leaned against the railing of the deck. Well, she tried there for a little while, remember? Bethany went back and forth, every other week."

"Yeah. Until she couldn't. But he didn't give her any choice. And for what it's worth, I think she made the right one, given the circumstances."

"I know. I do, too, but I sure wish it would have been different. For her. Did she say anything to you after she'd seen Bethany tonight?" Jen shook her head.

"No, not really. We just kind of left in a hurry. Don't blame her for that. And as you know, she didn't say much more tonight. Just that it was nice to see her."

"I know. I was dying to ask, but she didn't seem to want to say much." Faith gasped and pointed out over the waves. "Oh, look. A shooting star."

Jen followed to where Faith was pointing and saw the last few sparkles of the shooting star.

"Remember when the kids were little? We used to see them all the time. Now they're few and far between."

"Yeah. Too many lights now."

Jen realized that it was the first shooting star she'd seen all summer. Or at least she hadn't noticed any with so much going on trying to keep the beach house.

"I think maybe that one was for Carrie."

"That's a lovely thought. I bet it was." Faith hugged Jen and said goodnight.

Jen sat for a moment on the deck, the warm breeze tickling her neck. She thought she should turn in—it had been a very long day—but wanted to make sure Carrie was all right first. She wouldn't be able to sleep unless she tried.

The phone rang twice before Carrie picked up. Her soft voice offered a quiet, "Hi, Jen."

"Hello, dear friend. I was just checking on you. I know it was a really rough night. You okay?"

Carrie let out a sigh. "Yeah. I'm fine."

Jen paused for a moment. She knew that pressing Carrie wouldn't go anywhere, and she truly didn't want to pry. It was her experience that Carrie would bring it up if she needed—or wanted—to.

"Okay. I'm here if you need anything. And Faith and I would be happy to let the air out of Rob's tires if you think it will help. Or toilet paper his house. Or whatever you want."

Carrie laughed. "Thank you. I know you guys would. Just not necessary. It is what it is."

As Jen clicked off after saying good night, she remembered how hard it had actually been. When what it was was something completely different. Rob and Carrie, together. Carrie falling in love with Rob's infant as much as she did with him. And the crash that came many years later.

Jen's heart hurt for her friend, and the very public reminder of what might have been—but wasn't. Shame on Mrs. Westland for her selfish decision to invite them to something Carrie had worked so hard on. But knowing Mrs. Westland as she did, it wouldn't have been any other way. It still stunk, though, and just before she fell asleep, she wished her friend comfort and happiness. And as for Carrie's mother, she wished her something completely different.

FIVE

Ugh. Puppy breath. It wasn't remotely the way Jen wanted to wake up, but it only took a brief moment for Daisy's enthusiasm for a walk to infect her, too.

Jen stretched, threw on some shorts and a t-shirt, and headed downstairs. "Hang on just a second, Daisy," she said to the puppy whose tail was wagging furiously, her nose to the glass of the front door. "I need to start the coffee first."

She pushed the 'on' button on the coffee maker and grabbed Daisy's leash. The summer had provided some progress in puppy training, but not much. "Sit," Jen said, her hands on her hips.

Her command didn't elicit the desired response. Daisy was much more interested in the cat strolling by outside the door than in Jen's command. When she'd finally gotten the leash on the wriggling puppy, without Daisy's cooperation, Jen opened the door and tried to keep up as Daisy sprinted toward the beach.

Daisy spent as much time as Jen would allow trying to bite the waves, and Jen was grateful that she was wearing flip flops, wading into the water a little bit to keep hold of Daisy's leash. The water had begun to cool already, the sun a bit lower as the weather began to turn toward fall. She looked up and down the beach—families had already pitched umbrellas and set out coolers to enjoy the Labor Day holiday. At least this would be the last of it for a while, and Jen realized that this would be the first year that she didn't have to go back, too. It felt good—and strange at the same time.

They'd been so busy helping Carrie with the fundraiser that she hadn't been able to give much thought to what she'd do. She'd need to figure out how to generate some income, but she had a little time and she'd committed to her dad and her brother that she'd continue to fix-up the house—as cheaply as possible. On the cheap, she'd promised her dad. But she could do it. And it was time to pack up all of Nana's things and move them on. That would be a pretty big project in and of itself. Not a simple thing, to pack up memories that spanned a lifetime.

Daisy finally gave up her quest to bite a wave, and

she took off to see her best friend, Boris. Jen wasn't a bit surprised—Daisy would go every chance she could get—and today, Jen didn't mind.

"Well, good morning," Joe said as Jen and a very sandy Daisy approached his porch that looked out onto the beach. "Boris was hoping you'd stop by."

Jen passed through the gate with a nod to Joe. "He was, was he?" She dropped the leash when he shut the gate and laughed as the two dogs began to tumble on the small patch of grass next to Mrs. Russo's roses.

"Yes, he was," Joe said with a wink. "I'm not sorry you stopped by, either, but don't expect me to roll around on the grass to show it. Coffee?"

"Sure," Jen said gratefully. "Daisy pulled me out before I could have any this morning. Besides, yours might be better than mine anyway."

"Whoa, I bet that was tough to admit," he said.

Mrs. Russo pushed the screen door open with her backside, her hands full with two steaming mugs of coffee. Jen reached for the offered mug, and wondered at how Mrs. Russo always looked so sharp. Even this early in the morning her short, black hair was spiked with gel just perfectly, and her lipstick matched her colorful capris and complementary flowered shirt. She'd always dressed really nice, and Jen couldn't help but take a glance down at her own outfit that she'd grabbed from the floor of her bedroom.

"Thank you, Mrs. Russo," Jen said, her appreciation genuine and deep as she savored her first sip of coffee.

"You're welcome. Sit for a minute. How is Carrie? We were worried about you all since you left in such a hurry. That must have been quite a shock."

Jen nodded and glanced at Mrs. Russo. "It was. Did you have a chance to fill Joe in? He wasn't around for the implosion of their relationship, and I hadn't had the chance—or the reason, really—to fill him in."

Joe sat on the edge of the brick planter and sighed. "She did. Sounds awful. Who knew Rob would turn out to be such a putz?"

Mrs. Russo added her two cents. "Putz doesn't even begin to describe him. I could think of some much better words—"

"That's all right, Ma. We get the picture," Joe said with a smile. "I'm sure it's deserved, though."

Jen took another sip of coffee. "It is. No question about that. But I think she's okay. You know Carrie. She always looks at the bright side. Was just happy that she got to see Bethany at all, even for a moment. She doesn't talk about things like that much, but I know it meant a lot to her."

"Good grief. What a mess," Mrs. Russo said,

removing her red cat's eye glasses and pinching the bridge of her nose. "Her mother had no business doing that. But it doesn't surprise me one bit. That woman's always been horrible."

Jen's eyebrows rose. "Oh, you two know each other?"

One of Mrs. Russo's eyebrows rose as she peered at Jen. "Do we ever. We go way, way back. I have stories I could tell you—"

"Ma, maybe another time," Joe said, a half-grin spreading across his face.

Jen's curiosity was piqued, but any more questions would have to wait for another time as Daisy and Boris both laid down, their energy spent. If Jen had any hope of getting Daisy on their way home before she fell asleep, it had better be now.

She drained her mug and handed it to Joe. "Thanks for the coffee. It was great to spend the evening with you guys last night."

"It was a great evening, all things considered," Joe said. "Just sorry it was cut short."

Jen agreed, and an idea popped into her head. "We're having a barbecue for Labor Day. Should be some decorated boats on the harbor and Michael and Amber are coming out. Why don't you two join us? We can pick up where we left off last night, without all the...commotion."

Joe nodded. "Sure. Ma? How about it?"

"Well, I would love to, but I can't. I already said I'd go over to Back Bay Village to see Phyllis and watch the fireworks. They're having a golf cart parade, best decorated takes the thousand-dollar prize. Those people are nuts over there."

Jen agreed with that, too. The folks in Back Bay Village, just over the hill in the back bay behind Newport, were definitely living their own dream. Between paddle board races, tennis tournaments, bridge tournaments and golf cart races, she sometimes thought it sounded exhausting.

"Next time, for sure," she said with a nod to Mrs. Russo. "Don't get in any trouble over there. I've heard stories..."

Mrs. Russo waved her hand and snickered. "I never get in trouble, do I, Joey?"

Joe looked like he was having a hard time not laughing. "Well—"

"Psh," she said, with another wave of her hand. "Joey will be over for dinner and I'll send along a surprise."

"Thanks," Jen said as she clipped the leash on Daisy. "See you tonight, Joe."

Joe nodded slowly and opened the gate for Jen and Daisy. "I'll be looking forward to it."

SIX

Newport Beach was changing with the seasons, and Faith felt it probably more than either of her friends. It would be cooling off a bit from here on out, it being Labor Day weekend and all. School would also be starting, so the streets would be a little less crowded, and parking would get easier. And the purple ice plant would be in full bloom soon, covering the hillsides and beaches.

School starting. Faith sighed at the thought. The familiar jangling nerves had come early this year, and she wasn't exactly sure why. For the past—gosh, had it really been almost three decades?—Labor Day had been bittersweet. She'd loved her weekends at the beach and the long, dog days of summer had always gotten her ready for a new school year.

This year felt different somehow. Her decision not to teach summer school and stay in Newport to help Jen had paid off, she knew, and she was thrilled for her friend that the house would stay in the family. But every summer was fun, and she'd always looked forward to going back to her familiar classroom, meet her new group of kindergarteners and embark on a new adventure that would last until the following summer.

So as she found herself struggling to pack her bags— school would be starting the following week and she needed to go home and prepare—she knew she really needed to get on with it. She actually should have done it the previous week, but the allure of the fundraiser and the thinning crowds at the beach hadn't released her, apparently, because she was still there.

She gathered up the pillows that she'd made and set around the room, preparing to take them home with her. She'd sewn much of the summer and her handiwork was all over downstairs, too. Jen and Carrie had said that they made all the difference in the world in the living room and she did have to agree. She'd gotten pretty good at it. They were all unique—some with gold tassels, others with velvet inlay with crystal beads. She loved them all.

As she shook open a plastic garbage back to stuff

them in, she was startled by a knock and dropped them all onto the bed.

"I think you should leave those here." Jen stood in the doorway, a glass of wine in each hand and a slight smile on her face.

A slight smile was about all that Faith could manage as well. She reached for the glass of wine that Jen held out to her and plopped down on the bed with a deep sigh.

"You don't seem as excited for the new school year this time. You're usually knee deep in construction paper scraps by now. I haven't seen you cut out a single star for your new students."

Faith glanced at the stack of construction paper now back in her suitcase. Jen was right—she hadn't mustered up much interest yet. And that had never happened before.

"I don't know what it is, Jen." She followed her friend out onto the balcony of her room and leaned against the railing. The sun would be setting in not too long, but the sky had started turning into magical colors that Faith knew she would miss very much.

"I think I do," Jen said as she followed Faith's gaze toward the crashing surf.

Faith nodded. "It's been an incredible summer. I really feel like we got into a rhythm, and I've really loved working at the shop on the island. I really hate to give it all up."

"I know we haven't talked about this in a while, but is it possible for you to retire? I know you love teaching, love your kids, but maybe it's time to pull the trigger? You could stay down here as much as you want."

Faith pulled out a folded-up paper from her pocket and waved it. "This is my spread sheet of expenses. I've been going over it every single day trying to figure out a way to do that. I just can't figure out how to swing it. Not yet. Maybe another couple of years."

Jen nodded and walked back into Faith's room. "Well, it won't be the same without you around, that's for sure. I guess I'll have more time on my hands than I know what to do with. Who's going to do jigsaw puzzles with me?"

"Count me out," Carrie said as she bounced onto the balcony and re-filled everybody's wine glasses. "I hate that stuff. It makes my brain hurt."

"See?" Jen gave Faith a big hug. "What am I going to do?"

"What are *you* going to do? What's that crazy shop owner going to do without you, too? She's lucky to have you so she can go gallivanting all over the world," Carrie asked.

"Oh, right. What's her name? What did she say when you told her you had to go?"

Faith took in a deep breath. "She wasn't thrilled. Said she needed me, but I really don't have a choice. She offered to give me just weekends and my school vacations, but I said no."

"You said no? Why? That would be perfect," Jen said.

Carrie nodded and settled into the rocker on the balcony. "It really would. I'd love having you here, just like you have been all summer. It won't be the same without you."

"That's an understatement, but it's not all about us." She turned to Faith. "Don't let us pressure you, Faith. I know you have to do what you have to do."

Faith glanced back out toward the water. She had thought about trying to teach and working at the shop on the weekends, but it sounded a little overwhelming. Teaching kindergarteners was a lot of work, and Jen said exactly what conclusion she'd come to every time she'd allowed herself to think about it.

"And that would be pretty tiring, anyway. We're not thirty anymore."

"That's funny. We're not even forty anymore," Carrie chimed in. "We're not supposed to be doing stuff like that —working that hard, raising kids, wiping away tears. We should be on to the next adventure. The world is upside down."

Jen rolled her eyes as Carrie took Faith's hand. "Look, there's no harm in admitting our limitations. Or even our preferences. If you think it's too much, it's too much. But we sure will miss you for our Fantastic Friday Night happy hours." Jen leaned in a little closer, and whispered as she hugged Faith. "And I'll miss my room-mate. Please come back any time you want to."

"Come back even if you don't want to. We need you." Carrie looked over the balcony and said, "Oh, I have to go invite Mrs. Grover over for dinner, so I'd better get on it. Thanks for being willing to have her over. She really is sweet, you know."

Faith shared a grin with Jen. Carrie really seemed to have grown fond of the curtain-twitching neighbor when she'd spent the day spying on the open house a few weeks before. She'd been to visit several times since, and no one had objected when Carrie said she wanted to invite her to their Labor Day barbecue—even if they'd raised their eyebrows at the suggestion.

Jen had explained that Mrs. Grover and her Nana had been friends, even though Mrs. Grover was closer to Jen's mother's age than her grandmother's, and that she imagined Mrs. Grover had been a bit lonely since Nana passed, so they were actually all for it.

"Great," Jen said. "Michael and Amber will be here any minute and we have a farewell celebration to get to." She rested her hand on Faith's shoulder and smiled. "At least we have one more night."

Faith's heart tugged at the reminder, but she decided as this would be her last night in Newport for a while, she may as well do her best to enjoy it. Besides, Maggy had said she'd come, and Faith was looking forward to seeing her only daughter. It had been a while.

Carrie hustled back through Faith's room and rushed downstairs.

Faith followed Jen indoors and looked around the room she'd come to love.

"I mean it," Jen said. "Leave the pillows anywhere you want. It's your room, and it'll be here for you any time you want. Make it yours."

The soft, gauzy curtains she'd made for the room billowed in the warm, end-of-summer breeze after Jen left. Faith glanced at the stack on construction paper and then at the pillows. She carefully set each one where it had been—perfectly arranged to look their best in the changing light of the day—and nodded with satisfaction when she'd finished. She didn't know how frequently or for how long she'd be back, but she knew she would be. And it may as well feel like home.

SEVEN

Jen's mood lifted as Carrie opened the gate for Mrs. Grover, whose hands were full with a plate of cookies. She was growing fond of Mrs. Grover, and was pleased that she'd accepted the invitation. She caught a whiff of perfume as the older woman passed through the gate, and it reminded Jen of rose water, or something equally old and quaint.

The scent reminded Jen of her grandmother—not Nana, whose house they were all enjoying—but her mother's mother, who was much more prim and proper than her Nana had been. She wondered how Mrs. Grover and her Nana had been such good friends, when Nana had been such a free spirit and Mrs. Grover seemed—well, not that.

The comparison seemed even more appropriate as

Jen took in Mrs. Grover's black skirt and sensible shoes. It was a warm evening, but Mrs. Grover had on a lavender sweater, buttoned at the top, and her hair in a bun at the nape of her neck. It looked, to Jen, very uncomfortable, even severe.

"Your Nana's favorite, snickerdoodle," Mrs. Grover said with a wide smile as she handed the plate to Jen.

Well, that was one thing that Mrs. Grover and Nana had in common. They both loved to bake, and neither Jen's mother nor her maternal grandmother could even boil water.

"Aw, thank you," Jen responded, setting the plate in the middle of the table. She squinted at Carrie, who reached for a cookie but caught Jen's eye before she'd managed to snag one.

Carrie pulled her hand back and shrugged. "Can't blame me for trying. They're my favorite, too."

Mrs. Grover reached for a handkerchief from her sleeve. "I remember, from the day we spied on the open house. What fun that was."

Faith laughed. "I think they're everybody's favorite. But they'll still be there after dinner. And Carrie's grilling steaks, so we all need to be hungry."

"Oh, that's right. I'd better get on it," Carrie said, pulling out a chair for Mrs. Grover and heading to the barbecue.

"Carrie told me the news about Michael and Amber. My word, it seems just yesterday he was running around here in a diaper. I can hardly believe he's going to be a father."

Jen laughed. "That's exactly what I've been saying to myself. Seems like yesterday to me, too. I keep reminding myself not to say that to Michael. But I guess time flies."

Mrs. Grover nodded and rocked slowly on the porch. "That it does, my dear. That it does." She leaned forward and glanced down the street. "And here are the kids now."

Jen glanced down the sidewalk, her heart swelling at the sight of her eldest son and daughter-in-law. They'd announced that they were having a baby not too long before, and Jen couldn't wait to see how everything was going.

"Hi, everybody," Michael said as he opened the gate for Amber and ushered her inside.

"Oh, hello. It's so good to see you." Faith waited behind Jen for hugs.

"Michael, do you remember Mrs. Grover? From next door?"

Michael glanced at his mother quickly and smiled, nodding toward Mrs. Grover's house. Her lips quirked into a smile, and she knew full well he remembered her as the neighbor who spied on them and told them to keep it down at night. But true to form, he was polite and shook her hand with a slight bow.

"Good to see you again, Mrs. Grover. It's been a long time. You were a friend of Nana's, right?"

"Yes, a much younger friend of your grandmother's," she said as she nodded toward Amber when Michael introduced her. "And I hear congratulations are in order."

"Oh, yes, thank you." Amber blushed as she sat down on the porch. Jen hadn't talked to her much about the impending baby and looked forward to some quality time to do that. Unfortunately, tonight might not be the night—but she'd make sure they had time when it was right.

She really did love Amber, and had ever since Michael first brought her over. She was a perfect fit for Michael—a little bit quiet, but it balanced his gregariousness. He'd always been very outgoing, and they seemed to bring out the best in each other. They both had decent jobs, but she hadn't even been able to find out what they planned to do after the baby came.

"How are you feeling, sweetheart?" Faith asked when she sat down beside Amber.

"You look great. Positively glowing." Carrie rounded the corner with barbecue smoke billowing behind her.

She gave both Michael and Amber a quick hug and pinched Amber's cheek—which made Amber turn pink all over again.

"I'm okay, actually. I was a little queasy there for a few weeks, but it seems to have passed."

How had Jen not even known that Amber was having morning sickness?

Jen sat down beside her daughter-in-law and patted her hand. "I'm sorry, Amber. If I'd known, I'd have told you to eat soda crackers. I'm sorry I didn't."

"Oh, that's okay," Amber said with a smile. "My mom told me to, and I think it helped."

Jen felt a funny pull in her tummy that took her by surprise. She knew if she looked up, Faith would have a funny expression on her face, although Carrie would be oblivious. Faith knew much better the strange interactions Jen had had with Amber's mother.

Faith coughed before she said, "I'm so glad your mother was there for you, sweetheart," when Jen couldn't actually get the words out.

Jen thought how different it was to have a daughter—she just didn't talk about those kinds of things with her boys. It wasn't like they were going to get pregnant themselves, so she just didn't even think about it. Besides, boys were less forthcoming about all things emotional—at least in her experience.

Jen was grateful for the save—again—and decided it wasn't worth dwelling on. She made a mental note to check in more with Amber, so she'd know how things were progressing. But for now, she hustled into the kitchen when she saw the thumb's up sign from Carrie, the barbecue queen, and told everybody to take a place at the table. She was back in a flash with a tray of corn on the cob and a big bowl of Nana's famous potato salad. She'd go back for the watermelon next.

"Wow, that smells fantastic." Dirk Crabtree, the realtor who'd tried to sell the beach house and Carrie's fundraising partner, slipped through the gate and loosened his tie. Joe was right behind him, and he reached for the big bowls Jen was carrying and set them on the table after a hello to the other guests.

Carrie stood and smiled as Dirk climbed the porch stairs. "Well, thank you. I must say I agree."

"And from the looks of it, everyone else does, too," he said, glancing around the table.

"Please, Dirk, have a seat. We have plenty to eat. Join us," Jen said after quick introductions.

"Nice to meet you, Michael, Amber," Dirk said before flipping his tie over his shoulder and accepting the plate Carrie had loaded up for him—including the green salad that Jen had thrown together at the last minute, after her trip to the farmer's market.

"Thank you." He rolled his eyes in delight after his first bite, and Jen was pleased that he got to try the one thing that Carrie did know how to cook well—barbecue.

"I wanted to come by and actually apologize about last night. I had no idea that your mother was going to do that. Had I known, I would have done my utmost to stop her. What a zoo—and it can't have been much fun for you, Carrie. I'm really sorry."

Aside from Carrie's fork pausing slightly once on the way to her mouth, she had no other reaction. Jen wasn't surprised, but hoped that maybe Carrie would talk about it with Dirk. Unfortunately, she was disappointed.

"Oh, it was no problem at all. Truly."

Dirk stopped chewing for a moment and stared at Carrie, seeming not to believe her. The same sense Jen had.

"Nana's recipe?" Michael asked, helping himself to another scoop of potato salad.

Jen nodded, and Michael smiled even bigger.

"What happened?" he asked Carrie before he took another big bite.

Faith glanced at Carrie, but when Carrie didn't volunteer any information, Faith went ahead.

"Carrie and Dirk put together a fabulous fundraiser for Carrie's mom. It was great, and they raised tons of money for the children's wing at the hospital."

"It really was marvelous," Mrs. Grover added. "I haven't been to such a fun event in ages."

Michael rolled his eyes. "Don't tell me. Mrs. Westland did something cruddy and ruined it for Carrie. Right?"

Jen's eyes flew open wide and she nudged her knee into his—well, maybe it was actually a little stronger than a nudge.

"What? That's what usually happens. Why would this be different?"

Carrie sighed. "Michael's right—why would this time be any different. I should have known. It was too good to be true that we might come out unscathed."

"What did she do?" Michael asked, leaning forward. "I mean, if you don't mind talking about it."

Carrie just shrugged, and said, "It was really not a big deal."

Carrie sighed again, and Jen wished she could just make it go away, but it was probably best if she did talk about it anyway. She worried about her friend keeping everything all bottled up. But the cat was kind of out of the bag now, so she rushed in to try to help out her friend.

"She invited Rob, and Cassidy and Bethany."

Michael dropped his fork and stared at Carrie, blinking a few times before he said, "Oh, wow."

"Yeah," Faith said, looking down at her plate. "That's—that's—"

"It's fine," Carrie interrupted. "Really, fine."

Amber nudged Michael's elbow. "Who are those people?" she asked Michael.

"I'll tell you later," he responded, glancing at Carrie again.

"Oh, gosh. You guys act like somebody died. Amber, Rob is my ex-husband. Cassidy is his wife. And Bethany is my—was my stepdaughter. I just wasn't expecting to see them, that's all."

"Well, I should say not. After what he did to you, and making a grand entrance like that, with the Maserati and everything—"

Jen cut off Mrs. Grover before she could go any further, as Carrie's face was looking a little pinched.

"It was just gross. They could have just shown up without all that. I mean, if your mom really needed them to be there. For the attention."

"Oh, sheesh. I didn't put *that* part together," Dirk said. "So then, you're—um—I mean—"

Jen's stomach dropped, knowing where this was heading. And if there was anything at all she could have done to spare her friend the next part, she would have.

EIGHT

Carrie dreaded these kinds of conversations. Everybody always got so weird. And if she wasn't overly concerned, why should they be? She wasn't exactly thrilled that her mom had done that to her, but she was over it. She'd had to get over it—and quickly. No point dredging it all up over again. Past was past. But Carrie knew enough about this juicy topic first-hand to know that since Amber was just finding out about it, it wasn't going to die quite yet.

"Do you mean Rob and Cassidy from the Wives of Newport Beach?" Amber asked, her eyes wide.

Jen said, "Yep, one and the same. But it was a long time ago."

"Yes. I am the ex-wife that was on the cover of the tabloids for months. I am the ex-wife that he left for the bimbo with no explanation. I am the wife who was not allowed to go back to the restaurant that we'd built. Yep, that's me."

Nobody at the table quite knew what to say, Jen included.

"Wow," Amber said quietly. "I'm—I'm so sorry."

"Look everybody, it really is fine. It was just a surprise. I'm over it. Why don't you all have a cookie. Mrs. Grover worked really hard on those, I'm sure. And I'm tired of waiting for one."

She picked up the plate and passed them around with a big smile on her face. "On the bright side, at least I got to see Bethany."

Carrie was grateful that Michael recovered quickly, and helped her change the subject. Sort of.

"That's great. How is she? She must be—what, a sophomore school about now?"

"Yes, exactly," Carrie said. "I didn't get to talk to her for very long, but she said that they were on hiatus for the show and were going on a tour of the Continent."

Faith laughed. "She really said that? The 'Continent'?"

Carrie found herself laughing, too. "Yes, she did. I haven't heard that expression since—well, since I last read Jane Eyre."

"Neither have I," Jen said.

"That's weird. Why would she want to miss school?

Even the first half, or whatever? Is she still playing tennis? She'd miss the finals."

"Didn't get that far in our conversation. It was very brief. I couldn't really tell if she was happy about it or not."

"Hm. Well, did she seem good otherwise?"

"She did," Carrie said, nodding. "And it was nice to see her."

"And we got out just in time," Jen said with a laugh.

"Wow. Yep, your mom's a great wing-man, Michael. She tipped me off just before that lovely woman who married my ex-husband barged in."

All eyes turned toward the gate as it creaked. Carrie smiled at the sight of Maggy, Faith's daughter. It had been quite a while since she'd seen her, but there was no mistaking the lovely brown eyes, the wavy brown hair and easy gait. And when Maggy spotted her mother, those eyes lit up.

"Oh, my goodness, Maggy. We'd just about given up on you," Faith said as she rushed to hug her daughter. Carrie noticed again how much they looked alike, down to the kindness in their eyes.

"I'm sorry I'm late, Mom," Maggy said with a quick look at Carrie between hugs.

Faith reached for a plate and loaded it up, topped it off with a couple of cookies and patted the chair beside her. "No worries, we're just glad you're here now."

"Nice to see you again, Maggy. Been a long time," Michael said before he sat back down again.

Maggy smiled and nodded at both Michael and Amber. "I don't think I've seen you guys since the wedding, actually. It's been a very long time. And I hear you're expecting. How exciting!"

Amber blushed again and looped her arm through Michael's.

"Yes, and can't wait," Michael said, squeezing Amber's hand.

"Well, congratulations. The baby shower will be spectacular with these three." Maggie nodded at Carrie, Faith and Jen.

Carrie laughed when Jen took in a sharp breath. "Oh, my gosh. A baby shower. We'll have to start planning."

"Relax, Mom. You've got six months," Michael said with a laugh.

"That'll pass in the blink of an eye," Jen said.

Carrie leaned back in her chair as they all started talking about baby shower food, colors, themes. It wasn't her area of expertise, by any means, and she was grateful that the conversation had veered in a different direction. She'd never had a baby, let alone a baby shower.

Her memory cleared a bit, and she realized that that wasn't exactly true, and her thoughts turned to Bethany. She'd been a darling toddler—tow-headed, with piercing blue eyes that seemed to see everything, even then. She'd fallen in love with her almost before she'd fallen for Rob, she sometimes thought.

And her best friends had, in fact, had a small shower for her and Bethany. There'd been Beanie Babies everywhere, and Bethany had loved them. They'd had punch with orange sherbet in it—something she'd always hated, but had never told Faith and Jen that, even to this day—and they'd played games and giggled until they'd realized Bethany had fallen asleep in a pile of Beanie Babies, and Faith and Jen had helped get her into her crib.

She'd forgotten how happy they'd been, all those years ago. She, Rob and Bethany, just the three of them. They'd worked hard to start the restaurant, Bethany playing in her playpen while they planned and cooked—well, Rob cooked. Carrie never really learned how, but she was an excellent sous chef.

Everybody was so happy—everybody but Carrie's mother. Her mother, who'd never let her forget that Bethany wasn't her blood. Her mother, who'd never stopped asking if this was what she'd really wanted, someone else's baby. Her mother, who'd grinned at her from across the room last night, almost as if to say, 'I told you so.'

She felt a squeeze on her elbow and looked up into Dirk's questioning eyes.

"You okay?" he asked quietly, as the others were still yapping about the baby shower.

"Of course," she said, as brightly as she could, and wiggled her shoulders, shaking the memories off. None of it mattered anymore, anyway. It was all a long time ago. She really couldn't care less about Rob and Cassidy —they'd all moved on. And now Bethany had, too, and was heading to the 'Continent', giving up half a year of high school and an entire tennis season. But there was nothing she could do, anyway. Better to stay in the present, and the people she cared about were all right here.

Carrie glanced down the table—it was so nice to have everybody there. Max was the only one missing, and Jen had mentioned he wouldn't be home for another few weeks from his internship in Boston—and it was as if Jen had read her mind.

"Max will be back in a couple of weeks," Jen said, and she pointedly looked at Maggy, even though Carrie was positive that Jen didn't realize she was. Jen was never great at hiding her feelings, and most of the guests at the table knew that Faith and Jen had always hoped Max and Maggy would end up together.

Faith wasn't much better. "Right. He'll be back in a little bit. You'll be able to come up again, won't you?" she asked her daughter pointedly.

Maggy shook her head and smiled, with an exasperated look in Michael's direction. He returned the look and shrugged his shoulders.

"You guys really need to give that up. We already dated in high school, remember? No sparks, for either of us. You can't will it to be so."

Jen and Faith shared a quick glance, and both reached for another cookie at the same time. Carrie imagined it was probably to hide their disappointment.

"Well, you can't blame us for trying, right? We never give up on our kids."

Even though Carrie knew she hadn't given up on Bethany, the words stung. She wasn't exactly sure why—she'd done her best, and had never wanted to stop seeing Bethany. She hadn't had a choice. And she still didn't.

NINE

The sun had mostly set and the twinkle lights they'd installed around the top of the deck cast a soft glow on the still-tattered awning. Jen sat back in her chair, listening to her favorite people in the world catch up. She finished her glass of wine just as the sun dipped below the water on the horizon. It had been a marvelous summer, and this was the perfect way for it to end.

She looked around the table and soaked it all in. She hadn't been this happy in—well, she couldn't even remember. Max would be home soon, Faith and Maggy were together, and Michael and Amber were excited about the new baby—and the shower was set.

Jen caught Carrie's eye for a moment, and saw that there was a hint of sadness behind her deep blue eyes.

With all the commotion, there was nothing she could do about it at the moment.

She reached for another of the offered cookies, vowing to check in on Carrie as much as she needed to until she could get her to talk. She wanted all of her loved ones to be happy, so she needed to check in with Carrie and make sure it was so.

"Can we help clear the table?" Michael asked, standing and reaching for the plate of corn.

Jen stood and held out her arms as everybody passed her their plates. "Thanks, honey. I'll get the dishwater started if you guys want to bring stuff inside."

"I'm going to say goodbye, Carrie. Thanks for a lovely dinner, and it was nice to meet you all," Dirk said.

Jen waved goodbye and ducked into the kitchen when Michael held the door open for her. Amber followed with as many plates as she could carry, and Jen set about putting away leftovers as Michael washed and Amber dried.

"Can I be of service?" Jen turned as Joe came in, his hands behind his back. "I'm a pretty good dishwasher, but it looks like Michael is, too."

"I got this, Joe, no problem," Michael said, and Joe nodded.

"Ma said she'd send something, and she did." Joe held out a brightly-colored tin toward Jen.

Jen reached for the tin, anxious to see what was inside. Mrs. Russo was the best cook she'd ever met—except for her Nana—and it was bound to be good. She took in a quick breath when she opened it, and she glanced up at Joe who was trying hard to hide his smile.

"She thought you might like that. Spent the day in the kitchen before she went to her party. At least that's what she told me to tell you."

Jen laughed. "Oh, that was so nice of her." Jen couldn't believe that Mrs. Russo had remembered her favorite sweet—Italian wedding cookies, little bits of almond heaven covered in powdered sugar. "I can't believe she remembered."

"How could she forget? We stole them every chance we got, remember? The only thing that gave us away was the powdered sugar all down the front of you."

She felt her cheeks heat and she glanced at Michael —who had heard every word.

"Mom? Stealing cookies? Nah, can't be," he teased.

"Well, maybe once or twice," she said before she turned back to the leftovers, hoping that the pink in her cheeks faded quickly. "I remember that you and Allen did your fair share of sneaking into her kitchen, too, so don't pin it all on me."

Joe held his hands up. He reached for Amber's towel

and motioned for her to take a seat while he took over drying the dishes. "Fair enough. It was worth it."

Jen nodded and listened to Michael and Joe talk about—well, lots of little things. She was glad that she'd invited him—Michael had another opportunity to learn about his father, who had been Joe's best friend before he died. And beyond that, just talk to a man who was his dad's age—or the age he would have been. It warmed her heart, and everything seemed right with the world.

She boxed up leftovers for people to take home and got the rest of the things in the fridge, finally. When she was finished, she leaned against the kitchen counter. She folded her arms and grinned as she listened to her eldest son and his wife tease each other about who did dishes better. She'd worked very hard to make sure that her boys would be handy in the kitchen, and it appeared that she'd been successful—and Joe fit right in.

Michael took off his apron and glanced at his wife before tenderly resting his hand on her belly. "You okay? Getting tired?"

Amber nodded and sighed. "I am. I just don't seem to have much stamina at the moment. At least I've gotten my appetite back and haven't had to rely on saltines anymore."

"That's a relief," Jen replied. "You two can go ahead and head home if you want. We can finish up here."

"Sure. Thanks for a great dinner, Mom." Michael kissed Jen on her cheek, gave her a big hug and shook Joe's hand. "Oh, I forgot to mention that I stopped by the house yesterday and spent a few hours raking. The weather's gotten a little cooler, and there were tons of leaves that had dropped."

Joe whistled slowly. "You still have all those humongous eucalyptus trees that drop every leaf they have every day of the year?"

Jen and Michael nodded at the same time.

"Yep, the same ones you and Allen used to climb and almost give me a heart attack."

"Had to be done." Joe laughed when Jen lightly flicked him with a towel.

"She'd never let me climb any of the trees," Michael said with an exaggerated frown.

"No, and I still won't. Besides, you have Amber to look out for. No climbing of fifty-foot trees."

Amber agreed, then said, "I went with him and cleaned the inside. Well, I did what I could—dusted, vacuumed."

Jen stared at them in surprise for a moment. "Oh, I would never have expected you to do that. Amber, you shouldn't be vacuuming," she said, wrapping Amber in a hug.

Amber smiled. "It was no problem. Maybe that's why

I'm a little tired today. But it was fun. The house is so beautiful, and we knew you hadn't been home for a while. Thought it might need a little TLC. We opened the windows, aired it out."

Jen was so touched. She knew Michael loved the house—the one he'd grown up in—and she was grateful for the help.

"From what I remember, just the property is a lot of work. You're right. But you should have seen it when they were building the place. Quite a sight to behold."

Both Michael and Amber seemed to get a second wind as Joe described how Jen and Allen had built the house mostly with their two hands—both stories, with the vaulted ceilings.

"Your mom was queen of drywall, and Allen could build just about anything."

By the time he was done, Jen was immersed in the memories of long ago, and she had to shake her head once or twice when Michael said it was time they get going—long after they'd originally planned.

Back on the porch, Michael said his goodbyes, and Mrs. Grover stood to do the same.

"Nice to see you all again." She turned to Joe. "I'm sorry your mother wasn't here. I had a nice time talking with her at the fundraiser."

"She had a good time, too. She had another commitment tonight or would have been here. At Back Bay Village, for their Labor Day party."

Mrs. Grover's eyebrows rose as she looked from Joe to Jen. "Back Bay Village? Those people are pretty wild over there." She twisted her fingers together and looked worried. "You sure she'll be all right?"

Joe laughed. "Sure. She's just going to watch the parade and the fireworks. She can hold her own."

"Hm," Mrs. Grover said as she walked through the gate. "Well, thank you for a lovely evening. Enjoy the cookies." She walked quickly back to her house, with a last worried glance over her shoulder before she went inside.

Carrie laughed and shrugged her shoulders. "I wonder what that was about."

"Who knows?" Jen said. "But I have no doubt Mrs. Russo can hold her own just about anywhere. Right, Joe?"

"Absolutely no question," he said. "Ma's been around the block a time or two. She'll be fine."

TEN

The streetlights had been lit for hours by the time Maggy stretched and said she needed to head home. Everyone had left but Carrie and Jen, and they'd already gotten out leftovers to nibble on with the last of their wine, all of them excited to catch up with Maggy.

But now it was over, and Faith would be heading back to work tomorrow herself. It was a bittersweet end to a perfect summer, and she tried to remember how happy she was as she stood to walk Maggy to her car. Every time they got together anymore, Faith knew it would come to an end much too early for her, and every time it tugged at her heart.

She smiled as Maggy got warm hugs from Carrie and Jen, her 'bonus moms' as she called them. All the kids did, and she figured they must have done something right. And they were all close friends, too—Jen's Michael and Max, and Faith's Maggy—even if they weren't meant to be any more than that. Couldn't blame them for trying.

Maggy reached for her mother's hand as they headed down the sidewalk to her car, and Faith vividly remembered the first time it had ever happened—her heart had almost burst with joy, even though Maggy could barely walk at the time. So by the time they got to Maggy's car, it was hard for her to let go.

"Thank you so much for coming, Mags. It was so, so good to see you, and to hear about how great your job's going. I'd say who knew you'd end up working with numbers, but I guess we all did."

Maggy laughed and kissed Faith on the cheek. "I don't know. Maybe it was the way I turned everything into a math problem when I was little."

"That, or you telling me I could borrow a dollar if I paid you back two."

They both always got a giggle out of that story, and it was the same this time.

Maggy squeezed Faith's hand when they got to her car and shook her head slowly. "That's pretty rotten what Carrie's mom did. I guess we shouldn't be surprised but, man, that's pretty over the top, even for her."

Faith closed her eyes for a moment, then glanced

back at the beach house where Carrie and Jen were still chatting.

"I couldn't believe it. I really couldn't. But at least she got to see Bethany, and I think that was all she cared about. It's been a long time, and I know she misses her."

Maggy nodded. "I miss her, too. She hasn't called in —gosh, I guess it's been a couple years. And she stopped returning my calls a long time ago. I tried to keep in touch, invited her down for weekends, but she didn't want to come."

"I know, honey. We all tried. Just know that you were the best babysitter she ever could have had."

Maggy laughed. "Well, I don't know about that, but we did have fun when I'd babysit. I wonder if she still plays Scrabble. We were really good at it."

Faith laughed. "I doubt it. She looked so grown up. You wouldn't have recognized her. And dressed to the nines, just like Cassidy."

"Ugh. The Bethany I know would never have agreed to that. Sneakers, yes. Formal gown, no. But I guess people change."

"I guess so," Faith said quietly, with another look back at Carrie on the deck.

If Faith could have, she would have kept Maggy there talking longer, not wanting to say goodbye. But Carrie and Jen had asked all the questions Faith wanted to know about, so it was time to let her go. No guy in the picture, no dating at all, just her adult softball league and beach volleyball on the weekends. Maggy had played in high school, and continued on after college in a league in San Diego. Faith went down on the weekends to watch at much as she could, but hadn't been able to much this summer.

"I hope to get down for a volleyball game soon," Faith said as Maggy unlocked her car.

"Oh, no worries. I know you're busy, and I sent you a pic of the trophy we won."

"Yep, add it to the collection," Faith said before she wrapped Maggy in a big hug. "I love you, honey."

"I love you, too, Mom. Sounds like everything's great with you."

"Yeah, I guess it is. This job at the store on the Island and making all these pillows was giving me a run for my money, but I think I've decided to try to keep it up once school starts, If busy hands are happy hands, I'll be the queen of it."

Maggy smiled her bright smile and gave her mom one last hug. "It's great to see you so happy, finally."

As Maggy drove off and Faith continued to wave until she turned the corner onto Newport Boulevard, Faith thought about those last words. She knew that the last few years had been tough—her break-up with

Maggy's father had been less than amicable—and it had been hard on Maggy, too.

She sighed with relief that Maggy seemed happy—a lovely, confident young woman with a great job, a happy life. So maybe it hadn't been all that horrible after all. And as she turned back toward the beach house, she realized that she was, in fact, happy. Finally.

Now to figure out how to juggle all these balls she'd launched—a full time job teaching kindergarten, a weekend job at a store with a very unpredictable owner, a pillow project of her own. She hoped that she could keep all the balls in flight—and keep the life she'd worked so hard to repair on steady ground.

She looked back at where Maggy had just been, and then up on the deck at Carrie and Jen. She couldn't imagine never being able to see Maggy again, and hoped that Carrie was actually doing as well as she said she was. For Faith, it would have crushed her to have it all end that way and lose her daughter. She hoped that what Carrie was telling them wasn't all just delusion, and that she wasn't kidding herself.

ELEVEN

Carrie and Jen were pouring flutes of champagne when Faith got back to the deck. Jen handed her a glass and said it was time for a toast.

"Let's raise our glasses to the best summer ever," Jen said, the soft breeze from the ocean tickling their faces. She took a quick glance at Carrie. "With the exception of last night, of course."

Carrie shrugged. "Truly, I'm over it. This has definitely been the best summer in years. Saved the beach house, got to have Faith full time—we've had lots of fun."

"Definitely. And Joe's back, too. And Mrs. Grover and Mrs. Russo are hilarious," Carrie said after a sip of her bubbly.

Jen wiggled her eyebrows at Carrie. "And Dirk's not

too shabby, either. Glad he came by. He seemed really worried about you."

Carrie shrugged. "He's sort of nice. He's still a little bit too Mr. Newport for me, though. He knows every-body, always looks just right, and a realtor. You know how they are. I'm just glad we got through the fundraiser without too much collateral damage."

Faith and Jen exchanged a glance. "Speaking of collateral damage, have you talked to your mother?"

Carrie shook her head. "Absolutely not. I turned my phone off last night when I got home, and haven't turned it back on yet. No telling if she called. It's not like she's going to feel bad or anything. I just don't want to deal with it."

"I can't imagine doing that to one of my kids. Or any of the ninety-nine cruddy things she's done to you that I've witnessed with my own eyes," Jen said.

Carrie leaned against the railing and looked out at the waves. The wind had come up, and the waves had gotten bigger just since they'd finished dinner and crashed against the shore louder than they normally did.

She turned back to her friends and said, "You know, I used to spend a lot of time wondering about it myself. I remember I even asked my dad once. I couldn't figure out why she seemed to take pleasure in messing things up for me. Or at least making things harder than they needed to be."

Jen hadn't heard this before from her friend, and her ears perked up. "You did? What did he say?"

"I don't know. I can't really remember. It didn't make sense to me at the time, so I guess I just didn't think about it anymore. I pretty much checked out, and just did what she said until I could leave."

Jen couldn't imagine a mother not liking her own child. Just couldn't really wrap her brain around it. "You really have no idea? Maybe it's not against you—maybe she's just selfish."

Carrie took her last sip of champagne and set her flute on the table. "I don't know, and honestly, I don't care anymore. I shouldn't have agreed to help her with the fundraiser, anyway. Things had been kind of okay for a few years—okay for us, anyway—but I should have known better. Won't make that mistake again."

The blood in Jen's veins heated up. "I'd poke her in the eye for you if I could."

Carrie laughed. "I know you would, but today you'd have to stand in line behind me. Hopefully, tomorrow we can go back to pretending each other doesn't exist." Carrie crossed the deck and gave Jen and Faith hugs. "Thanks for being such great friends, guys. I don't know what I'd do without you."

Faith finished her champagne, too. "Feeling is mutual. I'm sure going to miss you guys."

Jen shook her head. "I can't believe you're leaving tomorrow. I guess this is goodbye for a little bit."

The three friends fell silent as the waves crashed against the shore.

"I really don't want to go," Faith said slowly.

"And neither do I," Carrie said. "I've decided to stay. For good."

Carrie and Faith just stared at her for a moment, and Jen imagined they were having very different reactions. When they spoke, it was clear she was right.

"That's fantastic," Carrie said. "I'm thrilled."

Faith looked as if she could barely muster up a smile. "I'm happy for you, Jen. But sad for me."

She looked as if she was mulling something over in her head, and Jen waited for her to continue.

Faith finally said, "It's only for a week. I'll be back on Friday. I'm hoping I can get all my school work done during the week and spend every weekend here. I'm going to try to keep the job at the shop. I don't want to miss any Friday night happy hours."

"Good. We're counting on you," Carrie said with one final hug for Faith. "I've got to call it a night, guys. Safe travels, Faith, and I'll see you next weekend. Good luck back in the classroom."

"You bet," Faith said as Carrie headed down the stairs.

Jen and Faith leaned over the balcony and waved until Carrie turned the corner onto the boardwalk, following the sand back to her condo.

After Jen was sure Carrie was out of earshot, she said, "You really going to be back every weekend? I'd be thrilled, you know."

"I don't know. It sounds like a lot, but I'll never know unless I try."

Jen lifted the champagne bottle up to the light and wiggled it. There was a bit left, and as this was Faith's last night, they shouldn't waste it. She poured the rest into their glasses and held them up for another toast.

"Here's to us all finding youth and stamina some-how. And to Friday night happy hours. And I wanted to make a toast to Maggy. She sure has turned out to be a really special young lady. What a treat to see her," Carrie said before clinking her glass with Faith's.

"Aw, that's nice."

Faith nodded. "It's true! How lucky are we that are kids are decent human beings? Kind, compassionate, loving. And Maggy is all that."

"And gainfully employed, all of them," Faith added with a laugh.

"That too," Jen said, and they clinked glasses once again as the wind calmed to more of a breeze.

After a moment, Jen said, "Bethany's tough, but she's a good kid, too. At least she was last time I saw her."

"Yeah, Carrie did a really good job with her. Put her heart and soul into it, too. I wish it had turned out differently for her. For them."

"Same here. I wish there could be some peace for them, too."

The two friends sat for a while longer and finished their champagne, but soon they both yawned and decided to call it a night.

"Sweet dreams," Faith said before she headed up the last flight of stairs to her room. "Thanks for a great summer."

"Good night, Faith. Thanks for pitching in and helping save the house. It was definitely a great summer, and I feel like it's really a new beginning. For all of us."

TWELVE

Carrie took her time walking home, listening to the waves crashing on the beach. It was breezy, but not too bad. Worth it to hear the waves crash rather than lap at the shore—and she was feeling like it was kind of a crashing waves kind of night.

She was glad that she hadn't been the focus of the evening too much—but it had always come back to her, somehow. The whole evening was something that she was just trying to forget about, but she appreciated her friends' concern.

It had been quite a shock to see them, if she was honest with herself. Well, to see Bethany, anyway. Rob and Cassidy looked the same—him preening like a peacock, as usual, and her lapping it up, diamonds dripping everywhere. She was actually pretty—something

Carrie didn't normally like to admit—but they were such gross people that it didn't even help.

But Bethany looked beautiful. When Carrie first saw her, she'd literally lost her breath. It had been several years, and now she was sixteen. She looked so grown up it had brought tears to her eyes. To Carrie, though, she could still see that little baby that she'd fallen in love with shining through her crystal blue eyes.

She tried to shake it off as she neared her condo. None of it mattered, really, anyway. Not even what her mother did. The fact remained that she still had no relationship with Bethany, and she still didn't want one with her mother. She'd learned her lesson. Tomorrow, she'd head back to her dental practice and immerse herself in work. Business as usual. And since she loved her job, it should dull a bit of the ache in her chest that she'd been trying to deny.

She'd known she'd be back after dark and had flipped on the porch light before she left. As she neared her front door, she stopped dead in her tracks at the sight of a beautiful bouquet of flowers sitting on her stoop. She ran over the events of the past couple days as quickly as she could, wondering who would send flowers. It wouldn't be Bethany. Certainly wouldn't be her mother. They must be from Faith and Jen, and she smiled at the warm thought. Everything in her world could be really bad, but Faith and Jen were her rocks, her bright spot.

She picked up the glass vase and leaned in to sniff the stargazer lilies. The scent washed over her and followed her into the room, and she set them on her kitchen island. The white baby's breath tucked into the flowers made them stand out even more. It really was a beautiful bouquet, and they made her feel much better.

The digital clock on the microwave told her it was too late to call Jen and Faith to thank them. They'd said they were going right to bed when she left as Faith had an early call to head inland the next day. She'd just read the card and call both of them tomorrow, thank them for being the best friends in the entire world.

Her phone buzzed, and she looked around for it. She'd completely forgotten she'd left it at home when she'd gone to Jen's—anybody she wanted to talk to would be there, so why bother?

The display read 'Jen' and she smiled, glad she could thank her so soon.

"I just wanted to check and make sure you got home all right," Jen said when Carrie picked up.

"I did, and thanks for the great surprise. The flowers are gorgeous. So thoughtful of you guys."

The phone was silent for a minute, and Carrie finally said, "Jen? Thanks for the flowers."

She could hear Jen clear her throat. "I would love to say you're welcome, but I didn't send them. I wish now that I had. That would have been very thoughtful of me. But I didn't."

Carrie turned to look at the flowers and narrowed her eyes. "You didn't? Not Faith, either?"

"No, I don't think so. She would have told me. We were very wrapped up in the barbecue. I'm sorry."

Carrie shook her head. "No, don't be silly. No worries."

"Well?"

"Well, what?"

"Who are they from, then?"

"Oh," Carrie said with a laugh. "I don't know."

"Carrie, check the card. I'll wait," Jen said, her voice incredulous.

"Okay, fine." Carrie had closed the books in her head on the past couple of days, and if the flowers weren't from Jen and Faith, she wasn't sure she wanted to know who they *were* from.

She plucked the card from the flowers and took a big sniff before she opened the envelope.

"They're very pretty, if you want to know."

"I'm sure they are," Jen said. "Quit stalling. Open the card."

Carrie sighed and opened the envelope. Her

eyebrows rose when she read it. She cocked her head and looked over at the pictures on the mantle.

"Carrie, you're killing me here," Jen said, bringing Carrie back to the present.

"They're from Dirk."

"Ooh, la la." Carrie could just picture Jen wiggling her eyebrows.

Carrie laughed and said, "The card says thank you for your help with the fundraiser, and I'm sorry it didn't turn out better for you."

"Well, that's nice. I still think it's an 'ooh-la-la', though. He sits awful close to you, if you haven't noticed."

"No, I haven't noticed. I think it's your imagination."

"Mh-hm," Jen said. "Well, either way that was very nice of him. I'm right, though."

Carrie and Jen arranged to take Daisy for a long walk on the beach the next night after work, and Carrie took in a deep breath after they'd hung up.

"What a couple of days," she said out loud to absolutely no one. An awful lot had happened, and the last thing she needed to think about was Dirk. Besides, she was one hundred percent positive that Jen was mistaken. They were friends—they got along well, and they'd just pulled off a big event. That was it. Mr. Newport was probably just used to doing things like that. For clients.

She changed into her pajamas and boiled some water for tea. She almost fell asleep as she let the tea steep, and grabbed the mug. Setting it on her nightstand, she didn't even make it long enough for it to cool before she gave in, and drifted off to a place where she didn't have to worry. About anything.

THIRTEEN

"I can't believe this is it," Jen said as she grabbed one of Faith's bags and followed her out the door with a paper bag in her other hand.

They'd had coffee on the deck early, and watched the sun light up the beach. But now it was the time they'd been dreading all summer.

"It's not 'it'," Faith said with a smile. "I'll be back Friday night for happy hour."

Jen knew she was moping, but she didn't want to make Faith feel bad.

"I know. I'm just going to miss you. What will I do without you?"

Faith laughed and put her bags in the trunk of her car. "You're going to go through all of Nana's stuff, remember? And then over the weekend, we're going to go decide what to move on. That's going to take you quite a while. And we can't start fixing things up until you do it."

"Right," Jen said. "But it'd be more fun with you here. Who will I talk to?"

"Oh, brother. Carrie's here, and I am absolutely positive Joe will be stopping by a fair amount."

"What do you mean? He's busy with work."

"Uh-huh. To use your favorite phrase, 'ooh-la-la'."

"Oh, my gosh," Jen said, and she couldn't help laughing. "I said the same exact thing to Carrie last night when she called about the flowers."

"And I know I'm right."

Jen almost doubled over, laughing so hard. "I said that, too."

"I bet you did," Faith said, her smile wide. She grabbed Jen in a hug. "I can't wait to hear all about it on Friday."

"Right. Sure. Oh, here, I made these to take with you."

Faith opened the bag and took a big sniff. "Nana's muffins! And they smell like buttermilk spice, my favorite."

"Yep. Enjoy. And good luck at work. Call me if you can," Jen said, and she waved all the way until Faith turned the corner.

"Well, Daisy, I guess it's just you and me," she said to the puppy as her tail pounded against the wooden slats of the fence.

She took Daisy for a quick walk around the block but didn't want to take her all the way to the beach, as much as Daisy tugged in that direction.

"Not this morning, girl. We're going to go tonight with Carrie. I've got a lot of work to do," she said as they made it back to the house. She took a moment to cut some of Nana's flowers and put together a quick bouquet for the kitchen counter—some alstroemeria and daisies. Then she set to work in Nana's closet.

Her grandmother had always been a snazzy dresser, but Jen had no idea how many designer things she'd had —from scarves, to coats, to sequined dresses. When she was growing up, she'd seen her grandmother mostly in skirts and capris, and had never seen any of this.

She pulled out a Hermes scarf and shook it out—the color of the flowers was still deep and crisp. She walked over to the mirror and flipped it over her hair, tying it under her chin. She reached for a pair of sunglasses— she'd found a drawer full of them—and tried them on, too.

A quick knock on the door called her attention, and she laughed at the look of surprise on Joe's face when she opened it.

"Oh, hello. You must be Audrey Hepburn. I'm looking for Jen. Is she here?"

She pulled off the glasses and stuck out her tongue at him, opening the door for him to come in.

"Very funny."

"No, seriously, you look like one of those beautiful gals in the movies in the fifties. Audrey Hepburn isn't that far off."

Jen pulled off the scarf, the smooth silk slipping through her fingers. "They sure were glamorous, weren't they? With these scarves and big glasses, you kind of can't help but feel you need to get in a convertible and cruise the boulevard."

Joe laughed and raised his eyebrows, pointing at a muffin.

"Sure, help yourself," Jen said, handing him a plate. "Buttermilk spice today."

"Mm," Joe said as he took the first bite. "It's delicious."

Jen loved it that people enjoyed Nana's muffins. It always made her happy, and now that she was going through her grandmother's things, she was glad she'd made a special batch this morning. Between the muffins and the flowers and the scarves, she almost felt like Nana was here with her.

Joe took a glance at all the scarves and coats that were draped over the sofa. "You sure have a lot, there."

"Yeah, I'm not even sure what I'm going to do with it. I think some of it was pretty expensive. This is a Hermes scarf, even," she said, twisting the silk between her fingers.

"That's very cool," Joe said between bites. "I can ask my mom. She knows about some consignment stores, or maybe you'd want to have an estate sale or something."

Jen leaned against the couch and looked at the clothes. "I don't know. Do people want things that are so old?"

"Are you kidding? They're not old, they're vintage. Getting a whole new life, from what Ma tells me. I can send her over if you want."

"Oh, that'd be great. Why don't you see if she'd like to come over for dinner? Both of you. I'm making Black Forest pot roast. The weather's cooled off a little and I'm ready to pretend it's fall. And I'm going to miss Faith, I'm sure. I'd be glad for the company."

"Ah, any kind of pot roast is great with me. Ma and I will be here if I have to carry her myself."

Jen laughed and wrapped up a couple of muffins for Joe.

"Oh, I almost forgot. This is why I stopped by."

He held out a tin. "From Ma. I told her you loved the cookies, and she said you could never have too many. So, here you go."

Jen opened a bag and grinned. "More wedding cookies? Awesome, thanks. Everybody ate the others last night, and I was kind of sad about that."

"Huh. I thought maybe you would be, so there you are."

"Please thank her for me, and let me know if you guys can come for dinner."

Joe headed down the steps. "Will do. I'll call her as soon as I get to work. Need to hustle at the moment or I'm going to be late. See ya, Daisy," he said as he headed down the street with a wave.

Daisy. Oh, right, she'd told Carrie she'd meet her for a walk and had already promised Daisy, and she wasn't likely to get off the hook with either one.

Well, if she hurried, she could get dinner in the crockpot early and be able to take that late afternoon walk with Carrie and Daisy anyway. That sounded like the perfect idea—she could have her cake and eat it, too. Or pot roast, in this case.

She laughed at herself and got to work in the kitchen, hoping that she could make anything half as good as what Mrs. Russo made. Fingers crossed, she vowed to give it her best try.

FOURTEEN

Carrie got up before the sun and by the time she'd finished her yoga practice, it was the perfect time to have coffee on the deck and watch the sun light up the waves. The wind had died down overnight, and now they were definitely lapping at the shore rather than crashing.

And that exactly matched her mood. A good night's sleep had cleared the cobwebs out of her head, and she felt great—ready to go to work, meet clients and move on.

She took a last sniff of the lilies before she grabbed her keys and headed out the door, writing herself a note on her phone to call Dirk later and thank him. It had been too late the night before, and she wanted to make sure she did it as soon as she got in.

As she was entering the reminder on her phone, a call

came through but she didn't recognize the number. She let it go to voicemail and was going to listen to it, but could tell in her call history that whatever number it was, the person had called something like ten times yesterday. If it was a number she didn't know, why would they call so many times? It was a local number, but it wasn't even remotely familiar.

She took a quick glance at her watch and realized she'd better step it up to get to work on time. Andrea, her office manager, came in an hour earlier to go through cancellations so things were under control, but she hated to be late.

Her phone buzzed again as she drove to work, but she'd put it in her purse and didn't really want to look at it. She'd enjoyed her calm morning and, after the past weekend, she didn't want to mess it up.

It didn't take but a second, though, for it to be messed up for her.

She wasn't even through the door before Andrea rushed out from the back offices, a stack of pink phone message sheets in her hand.

"I've only been here for an hour, and he's called twenty-five times. And there were more calls than that on the answering machine," she said, thrusting the stack toward Carrie.

Carrie took the stack and glanced at the number—

where had she seen that before?—but headed to her office to set down her things and put on her lab coat. She picked the stack back up and literally froze.

Rob. She flipped through the pink papers—Rob, Rob and Rob. And as she did, she recognized that it was the same number that had appeared so many times on her phone. What could he possibly want after all these years?

"You're going to call him back, right?" Andrea asked as she passed by the office door.

She stopped when Carrie didn't answer, leaning against the door jamb with her eyebrows raised and arms folded.

"Want me to call him and tell him to drop dead? Again? It's been a few years and it would give me great pleasure," she said, the corners of her mouths quirking up into a sly grin.

"No, I'll listen to his message and see what's up. I got this."

Andrea's expression softened. "You sure?" she asked, more quietly. Andrea had been with Carrie for years, and knew the entire situation.

"Yes, but thanks. It's all ancient history, anyway. I'm fine."

"Hm. Okay. Let me know if you change your mind. I

can help. It's not like I can get anything done if he keeps calling."

Her attempt at a joke was much appreciated, but didn't really help. Carrie couldn't even begin to guess what Rob would want to talk to her about. They had no financial ties at all, and since he'd made certain she couldn't see Bethany again, there really wasn't anything to talk about.

She picked up her phone and scrolled through her missed calls. Whatever was on his mind, he wasn't going to let it go. He'd called her cell phone almost as many times as he'd called the office...and left messages. It took almost ten minutes to listen to them all and for the most part, they were the same. "Call me. It's urgent."

His voice did get a little more strained with each call, though, and by the last one he got to the point.

"Bethany told me what happened. We need to talk about it. Now. Call me."

Carrie's stomach dropped for a moment, and her face flushed. So—they knew she'd talked to Bethany in the ladies' room. She leaned back in her chair and took a deep breath. There was nothing legal to say she couldn't talk to Bethany, only their agreement. And Bethany's clear desire. Yes, she'd taken a chance to just say hello. Things had cooled down after several years, and maybe she shouldn't have, but she did.

She did have a fleeting thought that she'd upset Bethany somehow, but she couldn't think of anything she'd said that would have. Their encounter had lasted less than a minute, anyway. What could have gone wrong?

Her intercom buzzed on her phone, and she pressed the button. "Yes?"

"He's on the line again. Want to take it?"

She paused for a moment, almost ready to say no, but she glanced out her open door and saw Andrea staring at her, nodding. "Just get it over with," she said.

"All right. Put him through."

She took in a deep breath and picked up the receiver, skipping all the niceties and hoping he would, too. "Hi, Rob. What's up?"

Apparently, he wasn't going for niceties, either.

He didn't even bother with hello. "This is all your fault, and I'm not going to let you get away with it. Bethany's a mess."

"Hold on a minute. What are you talking about? We ran into each other in the ladies' room. I said hello, that's about it." She didn't think he needed to know that she'd gone in to see Bethany on purpose. Probably wouldn't help.

"Oh, come on. You don't expect me to believe that, do you?"

"Well, yes. It's the truth."

She could feel him fuming through the phone, and she still wasn't sure why. "Seriously, after all these years, it shouldn't be a big deal to just say hello. What's the problem?"

She'd never known him to have a bad temper like this, and she was a bit taken aback. She didn't really care what he thought about her, but if she'd upset Bethany, she was truly sorry, so she decided to say so.

"I had no intention of upsetting her. I really just wanted to say hello. Is she upset?"

Rob let out a chortle. "No. She's happy as a clam. Why wouldn't she be?"

Carrie took in a deep breath and closed her eyes, gripping the receiver more tightly. She just wanted to end the conversation.

"Okay. Great, then. No harm, no foul. I've got to get to work. So, if there's nothing else—"

"Not so fast. She told me what happened. You said she didn't have to go on our trip to Europe. Why would you do something like that? We're supposed to be leaving Sunday night for a month. It's been planned for a year. She was okay with it, until you got involved."

Carrie leaned forward, her elbows on her desk, as she replayed the brief conversation with Bethany. She was positive she'd said no such thing. She had no right to, anyway. No custody, nothing. She'd just said hello.

"Rob, I said nothing of the kind. I was surprised to hear she was going, leaving the tennis team and school, but I said nothing else."

Rob barked at her again. "Well, that was enough, apparently. It took me months to talk her into it, convince her she could miss school and tennis season. Thanks a lot."

"I'm sorry you're having a problem, but I didn't say any of that. I'd be happy to clear it up if you'd like."

Rob paused for a moment, then said, "Great. That would be awesome. The camera crews are coming with us and she's expected to be involved. Besides, there's nobody to leave her with."

Ah, that explained it. Carrie had wondered why he wanted Bethany to go so badly—and it was for his benefit, not hers. Or Cassidy's. Figured.

She shook her head. Some things never changed. "Got it. Can't promise anything, but I'd be happy to talk to her."

"Great. I'll tell her to expect your call. She gets home around four."

"Fine," Carrie said before he hung up without saying goodbye.

FIFTEEN

Carrie went through her appointments for the morning in a daze. Fortunately, there weren't many complicated procedures, just routine stuff, but she was busy enough to not think about what she was going to say to Bethany. She'd have time for that later.

Andrea hadn't asked, and she hadn't really felt like talking about it. Granted, they hadn't had a moment without patients, but Carrie was relieved she didn't have to get into it.

Just as her last patient for the morning left and she'd checked the front desk to see what her afternoon looked like, Dirk came in. She'd completely forgotten to call him and thank him for the flowers, and she felt like a heel.

"Oh, my gosh, I meant to call you first thing this morning, before everything went sideways.

"No problem. I see you got the flowers. Sideways?" he asked, his eyebrows raised.

Carrie glanced at Andrea, who was leaning back in her chair and staring at her. She was sure that Andrea wanted to hear the answer, too.

"Yes. Rob called, and apparently Bethany is refusing to go to Europe. Says I told her she didn't have to."

Andrea leaned forward, her eyes wide. "What? You haven't spoken to Bethany in years. Unfortunately."

Carrie realized that Andrea didn't even know what had happened at the fundraiser—there'd been no time to fill her in.

"I actually saw her at the fundraiser.

"What?" Andrea asked, standing.

"Yeah. I had a one-minute conversation with her, and now Rob is accusing me of sabotaging the trip to Europe they're planning. Says Bethany told him I said she didn't have to go."

Andrea screwed up her face and waved her hand in the air. "Even I know that's ridiculous. You'd never do that."

Carrie shrugged her shoulders. "No, I wouldn't. But he insists that Bethany said I did, and is refusing to go. I told him I'd call her after she gets home from tennis practice."

"Whew. You sure have had a lot happen to you over the weekend."

"Yes, she sure has," Dirk said with a look of concern.

"All I did was surf," Andrea said. "I'd take my weekend over yours any day."

"So would I," Carrie said with a laugh.

"Hey, how about I take you to lunch? See if we can just let things settle down for a change."

Carrie turned to Andrea, who was already looking at the afternoon's schedule. "Good thing we book light on the first day of the work week. You've got plenty of time."

Carrie shrugged off her lab coat and gave Andrea a grateful smile. This had seemed like the longest day of her life, and it was barely noon. She wouldn't mind a little break, and it was nice of Dirk to stop by.

"Where would you like to go?" he asked as he opened the door of his SUV for her.

"I honestly don't care. My head is spinning a bit. I guess I probably just need to eat something."

"Well, we might as well make it something good," Dirk said as he pulled out of the parking lot of Carrie's building.

"How about Sol Cocina?" Dirk asked. "Fish tacos, maybe?"

"Perfect. I haven't been there in a long time," Carrie said, and the next thing she knew, they were heading into the restaurant. It was one of her favorites, but he couldn't have known that. It was authentic Mexican food, just as it was in Baja California, a place she had visited many, many times. She did her best not to think of all the restaurants she and Rob had visited when they'd been planning the menu at the new restaurant, and chose to remember the beautiful desert sunrises and sunsets instead.

Somehow, Dirk magically got the last seat by the windows, with the best view—which wasn't all that surprising for a Newport guy like him. The gentle ripples on the water were soothing, and she was grateful for the break.

Their waiter brought chips and salsa, and took their order. Dirk laughed when Carrie ordered the peel and eat shrimp, served with cotija cheese, lime and chiles. "I thought you wanted fish tacos."

"Me, too. But this is one of my favorites and I haven't had it in forever. Back in the day, we used to drive down the coast to Mexico, buy these and cook them on the beach. No way I'll be able to eat them all, though."

Dirk took another glance at the menu. "I've never tried them. Somehow, the name 'cucarachas' on the menu has never appealed to me."

Carrie laughed. "Maybe they think it's cute. But I agree, when you think about it in English, cockroaches don't sound very appealing. It's just kind of a slang term for shrimp down there."

"Hm. Well, maybe I should try some. How about if I order fish tacos and I'll trade you one for some of your cockroaches? My motto is to try anything once."

"Perfect," Carrie said, and she remembered she still hadn't really thanked him for the flowers. "I'm so sorry I didn't call this morning about the flowers. They're lovely, such a bright pink, and they smell fantastic. The entire kitchen smelled great when I got up this morning. Thank you."

"You're very welcome. Least I could do. I feel like I dragged you into this whole thing, anyway. 'How bad could it be'? I remember saying that. Well, I guess it was a lot worse than I ever thought it could be. And I'm sorry for that."

Carrie squeezed his hand. She felt bad he was so worried about her.

"Look, I knew it could be dicey going in. It took me a long time to even agree, knowing that my mom's primary concern is her standing in Newport, not her daughter's feelings."

Dirk dumped two packets of sugar into his iced tea and stirred, not taking his eyes off Carrie. "It must have been awful to have your ex and his wife arrive like that. Jeez, it was as if they were royals or something."

Carrie laughed and smoothed the napkin in her lap. "Honestly, that part doesn't bother me. Mother is so concerned about being the biggest fundraiser in the county that if I'd thought about it, she would definitely want celebrities there. And divorce was a long time ago. I really don't care anymore."

Dirk cocked his head and narrowed his eyes. "The divorce didn't shock you?"

"Not really. Aside from the surprise, we weren't really a good couple anyway. I mean, I was shocked when he ended up saying he was leaving me for Cassidy, but in hindsight, I shouldn't have been. We'd been living separate lives for a long time. Me and Bethany, him and his restaurant."

"Oh?" Dirk urged her to continue as he put a fish taco on her plate and took the shrimp she offered.

They laughed when they both reached for the extra-hot sauce at the end of the table.

"You, too?" he asked with a smile.

"The hotter the better," she answered, shaking the hot sauce onto her shrimp. "I need to apologize in advance. These are pretty messy," she said as she began to peel one of the shrimp.

Dirk smiled and nodded. "I see that. Good thing we have a lot of napkins. So, maybe when you split up, it was better that way. You had grown apart, it sounds like."

"Pretty much. And after we split up, it was fine for a while. It really was." Carrie took a bite of her shrimp and butter dripped onto her plate after it had run down her chin. "Oops."

Dirk laughed and eyed his shrimp. "You're right. They're messy, but delicious."

Carrie munched on a tortilla chip and looked out at the water. It was a beautiful day—the weather still gorgeous as Labor Day had just passed, even if a little cooler. Boats large and small bobbed on their moorings and she could almost ignore that further down the bay was Rob's restaurant. She turned back to Dirk and noticed he was staring at her.

"What?" she asked, after another bite of her shrimp.

"What made it not okay? You said it was okay for a while."

Carrie had thought she'd packed this all away. None of it was what she'd thought would happen. But Dirk seemed so interested, and she didn't have the heart to tell him she didn't want to talk about it.

She sighed. "We agreed on joint custody. I actually fought for full custody, as he was at the restaurant most of the time and I was the only mother Bethany had ever known, really."

Dirk started in on his fish tacos. "What do you mean?"

"Well, Rob and I met when Bethany was just a baby. Her mother had been young, apparently, and ran off with a surfer."

Dirk laughed. "I'm sorry. That's some poetic injustice, I guess. Hard to believe he'd do that to you after it was done to him."

Carrie had never thought about it that way, but Dirk had a point. "I guess so. Anyway, Bethany was twelve at the time, and I didn't get full custody as I wasn't her birth mother and hadn't officially adopted her. I was waiting until she was older and she could choose for herself, but if I had done it right away, things might not have turned out the way they did."

"Hindsight's twenty-twenty, I guess," Dirk said, wiping some salsa off his chin. Apparently, the fish tacos were as messy as the shrimp. "So, what did happen? If you don't mind my asking."

Carrie sighed, and decided that she might as well get it all out, tell him the whole story. She'd grown fond of him over the last few months, and he seemed like a nice man. And maybe it would do her some good to say it all out loud, especially if she was going to call Bethany later, and once again put her own heart on the line.

SIXTEEN

Carrie decided to let it all out, trusting that Dirk would be a good listener.

"Rob was adamant that we have fifty-fifty custody. But he wanted to alternate every other week. I think a week was about all he could handle. And that way, he'd have a week off with his new bride pretty consistently."

"I've heard of people doing that. In fact, my ex-wife and I considered it for our daughter when we got divorced. But she wasn't a very organized kid, and the divorce was tough on her. It wouldn't have been a good idea."

Carrie paused mid-bite and stared at him. "You have a daughter? How did I not know that?"

He laughed. "I guess we were pretty busy with the

house sale—or non-sale, as it turned out—and then the fundraiser."

"What's her name?"

"Abby." Dirk reached for his phone and got that proud dad look on his face that Carrie had seen—in other people. His smile was infectious as he flipped through a couple pictures, showing off a beautiful young girl about Bethany's age, with dark brown hair and bright eyes.

She was on a tennis court in one picture, and Carrie was about to ask when he said, "She's on the tennis team. She would have come to the fundraiser, but she had a tournament. Her mom took a video for me, though, of her last match and she did great."

He beamed like a proud dad would, and it warmed Carrie's heart.

"She plays tennis? Bethany does, too."

"She does. So do I."

Carrie couldn't help but laugh out loud. "Me, too, but I don't play much anymore."

"I don't either. Haven't had time, but I say we give it a go sometime. Could be fun." He smiled and set his phone on the table. "I'm sorry. I interrupted you. Go ahead. What happened when you tried to split custody?"

Carrie glanced back out at the harbor. "We tried that for a few months, and it required that Bethany pack up all of her stuff and basically move every Sunday night. We had duplicates of a lot of things, but not everything—school books, her favorite sneakers, things like that. It got to be pretty difficult for her..."

Her voice trailed off as she remembered the night she'd found Bethany crying in the bathroom.

"Oh, I'm sorry," he said, covering her hand with his.

"I contacted a counselor, and she asked a lot of questions. About things that I hadn't even noticed. And I realized that Bethany had stopped eating, and had lost a lot of weight. She had dark circles under her eyes, and I couldn't guess what was wrong."

"Ah. That's pretty much what we were worried about with Abby. She wasn't a very organized kid, either. That can be hard on them, moving every week."

Carrie nodded slowly. "I know. I mean, I know now. At the time, I thought it was a good compromise. Turns out, not so much. At least for us. I think some kids can handle it just fine—she just wasn't one of them."

"So what did you do?"

Carrie laid her napkin across her plate. She hadn't quite finished all of her lunch, but she'd lost whatever appetite she'd had.

"I told Rob what the counselor said, let him know I was worried about Bethany. That I thought she needed to have one house as her primary residence. You know, maybe see him every other week, and maybe all summer. The time would be the same, but during the school year she'd have a more stable environment."

"I take it he didn't agree."

Carrie let out a wry laugh. "Oh, he definitely did. But he decided it should be at his house, not mine. I didn't see that one coming."

Dirk's eyes grew wide, and he ran his hand through his hair. "Wow, that must have been a shock."

"It was. And as he was her legal parent and I wasn't, I didn't have anywhere to go with it."

Dirk let out a slow whistle. "What an awful choice. Why would he want to do that if he preferred the time off? I don't get it."

Carrie grimaced. "By that time, Cassidy had gotten her spot on the Housewives show, and Bethany was part of it. At least enough of a part where she needed to be around more when they were filming. Bethany thought it was fun for about a minute, but quickly lost interest. Cassidy didn't, though, and they needed her. It was really awful. There wasn't anything I could do." Carrie looked down at her plate and realized she was making squiggles in the salsa with a chip.

"Let me guess. You didn't let Bethany know that you'd tried to have her live with you full time, right?"

Her head snapped up and their eyes met. "How did you know?"

Dirk pushed his plate away and leaned forward, his elbows on the table. "Because that's what a mom who cared about her daughter's mental health would do, I think. If she was already having trouble, getting involved in a war between the two of you would have only made it worse."

Carrie paused while the waiter filled up her glass of iced tea, and topped off Dirk's.

"Well, that was my thinking at the time. What I didn't know was that she would feel like I abandoned her, and we would lose touch. She didn't want to come see me when she could—said it was too hard, and she had homework to do when she wasn't working on the show. I think I cried myself to sleep for an entire year. I couldn't believe she didn't love me anymore."

Carrie looked up again, and Dirk's eyes mirrored her sadness. "Hey, that's not the truth. That's not what happened. You're her mom. Teenagers—well, teenagers honestly are a species unto themselves, I think. It won't last forever. But I bet it was tough."

"It was," Carrie said, nodding slowly. "And seeing her the other day—I was just so excited. She looked miserable still, but she was a sight for sore eyes for me, that's for sure."

Dirk rested his chin in his hand as he leaned forward again, his finger tapping. "So, you're going to call her this afternoon to see what happened, why she doesn't want to go all of a sudden?"

Carrie nodded slowly. "That's what I told Rob I would do. I hope it goes well."

"You don't talk to her anymore?"

"Not really. I quit trying after about a hundred unreturned voicemails, over months. I send her an email once a week, but never get one back."

"I can imagine. Well, she's sixteen now, right? Maybe a little bit more mature?"

"I don't know. Maybe."

"And she doesn't want to go. And there's nowhere for her to stay."

Carrie stared at Dirk for a moment, then glanced over at Rob's restaurant. He had people who would cover there, and she hadn't said it outright to Bethany, but she really shouldn't miss fall semester and her entire tennis season. Last they'd spoken, Bethany was hoping she'd get a scholarship. And even though she hadn't been able to be there for Bethany in the way she'd wanted to before, she could now.

"I'm going to offer for her to stay with me," she finally said, setting her glass of iced tea with a thud.

"Oh, yeah?" Dirk said, his smile wide. "That sounds like it could get interesting.

"Well, Rob wants her to go, but I bet his bigger problem is that there's nowhere else for her to stay. And he doesn't want to give up his big trip—at least that's what I'm guessing."

"I'm sure that's about right. And you guys could spend time together. Get to know each other again. Play tennis." Dirk looked so excited he was almost wiggling in his chair. "It's brilliant."

Carrie smiled at his kindness and excitement on her behalf. Just the thought of Bethany coming to live with her lifted her heart. But Carrie wished a little bit more of his confidence would rub off on her. She wasn't at all convinced that Rob would allow it—or that Bethany would want to.

But she missed her daughter mightily, the other night had made that really clear. And after she and Dirk ran through some possible ways for her to get it out, she decided that it was worth a try. In all honesty, she had nothing to lose. There was no way things could possibly get worse.

SEVENTEEN

"When are you going to call?" Andrea asked when she returned to the office. "You have four more appointments, I think. Should be done by four thirty."

"Perfect. Rob said she gets home from school at four. I'll call after the last patient leaves."

Carrie shrugged on her white coat, scrubbed her hands and somehow got through her day. She'd tried not to be too hopeful, but even as she was working on patients, she'd daydreamed about all the fun she and Bethany could have, just like old times. Making popcorn and watching Gilmore Girls—did Bethany still like Gilmore Girls, she wondered? It might take a little bit to find out what she did like, but as the day wore on and she allowed all the happy memories they had to drift through her mind, her hopes were high.

She'd finally seen her last patient and hung up her white coat, and it was time to make the call.

"You okay?" Andrea asked, leaning back in her chair so she could see Carrie sitting at her desk, staring at the phone.

Carrie looked up and smiled, trying to gather her courage. After being steeped in happy memories all day, she wasn't sure how she'd do if Bethany said no.

Suddenly, Andrea was standing at her desk. She picked up one of the pictures of Carrie and Bethany and gazed at it, turning it so Carrie could see. "Just remember the girl you love, and do your best."

Carrie smiled gratefully and set the picture right in front of her. "Thanks, Andrea. I really don't have anything to lose, do I?"

"Nope. And an open heart is your best bet."

Carrie nodded and picked up the receiver. She took one last glance of the picture of her and Bethany—both in tennis outfits, big smiles and orange bows in their hair —and punched in the numbers.

Her heart skipped a beat when she heard Bethany say, "Hello."

She realized she hadn't actually planned what she wanted to say right beforehand, so she tried to remember what Dirk had helped her with.

"Hello, Bethany. It's Carrie." She didn't even know if

that was right. Bethany used to call her 'Mom' but that didn't feel right now.

"Hello, Carrie," Bethany said.

"It was really nice to see you the other night," Carrie began, wishing Bethany would help out a little but not surprised that she wasn't.

"Uh-huh," Bethany said.

Carrie tapped a pencil on her desk and stared at the picture. There really wasn't anything to do but do it, she supposed.

"Your dad says that you don't want to go to Europe now. And that I told you that you didn't have to."

She was met with a brief silence. "Um, yeah, sorry about that. I know that's not exactly what you said."

"No, it isn't," Carrie agreed, glad that honestly wasn't an issue. "So what's going on?"

"I guess I just got to thinking about what you said, and I really don't want to miss fall semester. Or my tennis season, either. I really like tennis. And I'm good."

Carrie smiled at her confidence. She was good. No reason to pretend she wasn't.

"You still thinking about maybe a tennis scholarship somewhere? For college?"

"I am, I guess. I've had scouts come to see me. Dad says it's not important, that I don't need a scholarship as they have more money than God."

Carrie stifled a laugh. That sounded more like Cassidy than Rob, but whatever.

"It's more fun in college if you're on a team. Easier to meet people. I still talk to my tennis teammates from college. They've become lifelong friends."

"That's what I was thinking. But he really wants me to go, and says there's nowhere for me to stay, anyway."

Carrie realized that it was now or never, if she was going to make the offer for Bethany to stay with her, and she gathered her courage.

"I've been thinking about that, too. You are welcome to stay with me. Any time. But especially now."

"Hello?" she asked after waiting a while with no response from Bethany.

"I'm here. I—I'm not sure about that."

"Oh." Carrie put the picture of them face down on the desk and rubbed her eyes. "I thought maybe we could have some fun. Like old times." Her courage faded, and she wasn't quite sure what else to say.

Bethany seemed to take another whole minute before she spoke again. "Well, I'm pretty busy in school. Between that and tennis, I'm not home a lot anyway."

"I can imagine. I remember how much time it takes."

"You have a bedroom for me?"

"Of course. And it's all cleaned out. Nobody's ever stayed in it, even. It's all yours."

This conversation was like pulling teeth. Not what Carrie had anticipated, but it had probably been a little naive for her to think it would go any other way.

"I suppose it wouldn't hurt, since I'd be gone most of the time. Just a place to crash."

"Um, well, if you want to think of it that way, I guess that's all right. I just wanted to be helpful."

Bethany let out a funny noise that didn't quite sound like a laugh. "Yeah, right. Okay. Thanks."

"You're welcome. See you Sunday, then, I guess?"

"I guess," Bethany said.

Carrie hung up slowly and shook her head.

"Well?" Andrea said, and Carrie was pretty positive that she already knew all of Carrie's side of the conversation.

"It wasn't exactly like she was jumping for joy, but she said yes."

"Man, teenagers. My sister has one and they're like aliens from another planet, in my opinion."

Carrie looked up, her eyes wide. She did remember that Maggy had given Faith a run for her money when she was Bethany's age, but Bethany was always a very sweet little girl. She was certain that she was just a little mad, and that everything would turn out okay as soon as she and Carrie could spend time together.

"I'm sure it'll be great. We can watch Gilmore Girls

together and eat popcorn. I can help her with her homework and meet her friends. Maybe play some tennis together."

She looked up and it appeared that Andrea was trying hard not to laugh, her hand covering her mouth.

"Yeah, okay. Spoken by the woman whose mother just completely ruined her weekend."

Carrie had tried very hard not to think about her own mother, who was never there for her when she was a teenager, nor remotely interested in anything she was doing. And she was determined to continue not thinking about her mother, and try to make it different with Bethany.

But her stomach felt a little queasy when Andrea said, "Teenagers can be a handful, Carrie. Be careful what you wish for."

EIGHTEEN

Carrie was still in shock that Bethany was actually going to come and stay with her, and she was so excited she just changed into her walking clothes as fast as she could and almost sprinted to Jen's house. She couldn't wait to tell her the news.

Jen was waiting with Daisy, who was trying to pull Jen as hard as she could down toward the water, and Carrie followed. After Daisy arrived at her destination and bit the waves for a few seconds, she took off down the beach, and Carrie and Jen fell into a rhythm behind her, the wind at their backs.

"You're not going to believe what happened," Carrie said.

Jen pulled her visor down more tightly over her eyes against the sun that had begun to set.

"Dirk stopped by the clinic today, right?"

Carrie stopped in her tracks for a second, then jogged to catch up with Jen and Daisy as Jen laughed.

"Well, yes, how did you know that?"

"Just a hunch."

"Okay, but that's not what I was going to tell you."

"Wow, something bigger than that? That's pretty big in my book."

Carrie nudged Jen with her elbow. "Stop. He's a friend. We went out for lunch."

"Oh, give me details."

"Stop. That's not the story."

Jen looked over at Carrie and smiled, but stopped teasing. "Okay, what then?"

"Bethany is coming to live with me. For a month."

It was Jen's turn to stop in her tracks and stare at Carrie. "What? You're kidding."

"No, I'm not," Carrie said as they both acquiesced to Daisy's tugging and started walking again. She spent a few minutes giving Jen all the details, and when she was done, Jen shook her head slowly.

"I would never in a million years have guessed that's what you were going to say."

"I know, right? I've been discombobulated all afternoon. Very excited. And nervous."

Jen looked at Carrie out of the corner of her eye.

"That explains why you're wearing plaid shorts and a flowered shirt, I guess."

Carrie looked down at her outfit and shrugged. "I wasn't paying attention. What's wrong with it, anyway?"

Jen laughed. "Nothing. So when is she coming?"

"Sunday evening. Rob's going to drop her off on their way to the airport. I can't believe he agreed to this. I almost don't know what to do."

"I'm so happy for you, Carrie. For all of us. It'll be great to spend time with her. Get to know her again. She'll be in school, mostly, and at tennis practice, no? Fall is tennis season."

Carrie bounced along on the sand. "Right. I suppose there'll be lots of tournaments. I can't wait to go watch. She was so good, even when she was little."

"Well, you taught her. Remember?"

Carrie did remember. They'd spent hours on the courts—chasing balls, mostly. Mostly, it had been fun to be outside, but she eventually grew into a very strong player. Even Carrie's mother had said so—once.

"Um, there's something else. I've got to clean out the spare bedroom. It's become a storage room over the years. Dang. And I only have the rest of this week. I told her it was already cleaned out and ready for her," Carrie said as the heat rose in her cheeks. But Jen just laughed, as Carrie knew her friend would.

"I can help. And Faith'll be here this weekend. We can spruce it up a little bit if you want, too. I haven't seen it in a long time. What does it look like?"

Carrie thought for a moment. She'd been in the condo for years, but never really paid attention to that room. She just stored stuff in it.

"It's white."

Jen paused for a minute. "White?"

"Yeah, white. You know, just white paint. What am I supposed to do?"

Jen shook her head. "For somebody who dresses so colorfully, your condo sure is bland."

Carrie hadn't really noticed. She had some family pictures up—well, of her dad and Bethany—and a couple colorful dishtowels. And Faith had given her some awesome pillows that she'd sewn over the summer. They even had beads around the edges.

"Okay. Guess maybe I need a little bit of an over-haul. Maybe we could do that this weekend?"

"Sure. Let's talk about it at Friday night happy hour on the deck. Faith'll have great ideas, I'm sure. Mean-time, "I'll just box things up and put them in your garage."

"Thank you. You're a lifesaver. I can help at night." Carrie thought for the millionth time how grateful she was for her friends. What she couldn't do, they could help with—and vice versa. She was grateful.

"I guess I'll need to go to the grocery store, too. I don't have much to eat at my house, either."

"I'm stunned," Jen teased as they passed through the gate of Jen's beach house. Jen let Daisy off her leash and Carrie followed her into the house.

"Oh, wow. What are you cooking? It smells great."

Jen pointed to the crock pot. "Mrs. Russo and Joe and coming for dinner, and I knew we were walking so I threw together one of Nana's old crockpot recipes. Want to stay?"

Carrie took in a deep breath and peered into the crockpot. Jen laughed when her stomach growled.

"I guess that's a yes."

"Well, if you seriously don't mind, I'll take you up on it. Like I said, not much to eat at my house, and I'm too antsy to think about it. It's been a big day."

Jen poured two glasses of red wine—Carrie's favorite —and said, "We have to have a toast before they get here. This really is a major event, Carrie. I'm thrilled for you. For both of you."

Carrie and Jen clinked glasses, and Carrie knew Jen was right. It really was a big deal. And to think that this morning when she'd woken up, she'd had no idea this would happen. Things sure could change quickly.

"How much time do we have before they get here?"

Jen glanced at the clock. "At least half an hour."

Carrie reached for her phone. "Let's call Faith. I want to tell her the news, too, and see how her first day was. We can FaceTime and maybe she'll want to have a glass of wine with us."

"Perfect," Jen said as she filled Daisy's food bowl, grabbed the bottle of wine and followed Carrie onto the deck.

NINETEEN

Faith hung up the phone and sighed. She couldn't tell what she was feeling most—thrilled for Carrie, jealous she wasn't with them on the deck or just flat-out exhausted from her first day trying to get her classroom in shape. But there was no doubt about the fact that she was thrilled for Carrie and Bethany.

It had been a long day for Faith. She'd hit tons of traffic on her way home from the beach, which didn't exactly surprise her. The Tuesday after a three-day weekend was always treacherous, but the drive that should have taken an hour took two. She hadn't even had time to unload her car—she'd driven straight to her school site. And even then, she almost missed the staff meeting.

"Welcome back, all of you," her principal had said to

all the faces in the cafeteria. As Faith looked around, there were more than a few people she didn't recognize and she felt like she'd been gone for years, not just the summer. Many of them were young and eager-looking, but Faith sat with the older, seasoned teachers she'd become fast friends with over the years.

Faith had heard this 'welcome back to school' speech many, many times and her thoughts drifted while her principal spoke. She wondered what shape her class-room was left in after summer school, and how much work it would take to get it ready. She wondered how many of the new teachers with fresh faces would last until the end of the year. And as she looked around the cafeteria, she wondered how many of her friends would declare that this year would be their last.

She loved her job, but she knew she couldn't do it forever. Kindergarteners were sweet, eager, interested— and very, very busy. Nonetheless, she was excited for the year to start, and she'd spent the rest of the day looking over her student roster, printing the names neatly on cut-out construction paper shapes and hoping that by the end of the year, they'd all recognize not only the letters of their names, but the entire alphabet.

When she'd gotten home, she'd made herself a cup of tea and sat with her feet up for a little while, not eager to unpack the car. But by the time the sun was a little lower on the horizon, she'd had another burst of energy, unloaded the car and poured a glass of wine. She looked around the kitchen, wishing Jen was cooking for her as she had been all summer. When the phone rang and she got to FaceTime with her friends, she was thrilled. And now that Carrie had shared her good news and they'd hung up, fatigue and loneliness washed over her once more.

She was just thinking she should let Maggy know the news about Bethany when the phone rang—Maggy's ears must have been burning.

"Hi, sweetheart," Faith said when she picked up.

"Hi, Mom. How are you doing? I thought it might be a big change for you after having been at the beach all summer, hanging out with Jen and Carrie."

"Aw, that's sweet of you. It certainly has been a big change, that's for sure. And we don't even have students yet. But the house here is pretty quiet, I'll say that."

"I bet," Maggy said.

Faith filled her in about Bethany, and she knew Maggy was as surprised as she'd been.

"Wow, I certainly didn't expect that. Not after Carrie's story last night. Things sure can change fast."

"You can say that again," Faith said. "I hope you'll be able to come and visit while she's around."

Maggy paused for a bit. "You said she's going to be

there for a month? I'm sure I can make it up to see her. That'll be strange, but great. I'll look forward to it."

"Great. All good with you?"

"Yep. Just checking on you. All good here."

"Thanks for calling, honey. I really appreciate it."

"No problem, Mom. I'm here if you need me."

Faith sighed when they ended the call. It was so nice to be able to talk to Maggy now, just like two normal people. And she remembered that it hadn't always been that way.

Her mind drifted to the time when Maggy was Bethany's age. It seemed to her that months had gone by when they'd barely spoken, and Faith couldn't do anything right, according to Maggy. But they'd made it through those teenage years, and when Faith and Maggy's dad had finally parted ways—which had been long overdue—she and Maggy were able to weather the storm without too much damage.

She hadn't thought about that for ages, and she hoped that Carrie and Bethany could enjoy good times together over the next month, and heal some of their older wounds. And that the teenage years for them were smoother than they had been for Maggy and Faith. All she could do, though, was keep her fingers crossed. And help whenever she was able.

TWENTY

Jen set down the phone and leaned back in her chair on the deck. "Faith looked tired, don't you think?"

Carrie nodded. "Yes, she did. But she had a pretty long day."

"I guess we all did. But I can't imagine working in a classroom with kindergarteners, can you? Getting the classroom ready, planning for the year. It sounds over-whelming."

"It does to me, too. It's much easier to just take x-rays and meet with patients all day. You wouldn't think so, but it is."

"Yeah, but both of you guys love your jobs."

"We do, and you get to go through your Nana's stuff and figure out what to do here. And we know Faith loves what she does."

"I suppose everything is pretty good right now, if you think about it."

"What a nice thing to hear," Mrs. Russo said as Joe opened the gate for her. "That's how life should be. Happy."

Jen gave Mrs. Russo a quick hug and took the bottle of chianti Joe held out to her. "Thanks, Mrs. Russo. We were just thinking the same thing."

"Something smells delicious, Jen."

"Thanks. It's one of Nana's recipes and I have to say, it's made the house smell great all day."

"I think Mrs. Grover might agree," Joe said, his thumb gesturing toward the neighbor's window just as the curtain fell shut again.

"Oh, good grief. She's something else," Carrie said with a laugh. "Mind if I invite her? She's sweet."

Jen nodded as she opened the door and ushered everybody in. "Absolutely not. Go get her."

Joe helped set the table as Mrs. Russo poured the chianti. "Thanks for the invitation. I'm sorry I couldn't come last night. We had that big shindig over at Back Bay Village. Good grief, those people are something else."

Jen started plating the pot roast, and handed Joe a spoon to add the broccoli and mashed potatoes. He knew exactly what to do, and it was turning out that they worked well together in the kitchen. "What do you mean?"

Mrs. Russo waved her hand. "Well, it's just an interesting senior community. They're small homes, and a lot of them right on the water. It's been there forever. None of them would be able to afford houses in Newport now, but some of them have been there for thirty, forty years. There are tennis courts, a pool, a big community center. And they all have duffies, those little electric boats, that they take out in the bay. They even have races. And one lady told me she takes hers out and they have Farkle parties on it."

"Farkle?" Jen asked, her eyebrows raised.

"Oh, it's a dice game. And I think it involves drinks."

Jen laughed. "I love those electric boats," Jen said. "We have one, but it's not working at the moment."

"I'd be happy to take a look at it," Joe said as they set the plates down on the table.

"Thanks, that would be awesome." Jen set the gravy down on the table and glanced out the window, looking for Carrie and Mrs. Grover.

"Not sure what happened to them."

Joe poked his head out the door, then held it open wide. "Here they are. Just in time, you two.

"Thanks. We got hung up for a minute. Mrs. Grover was showing me her vintage jewelry collection. I'm not all that knowledgeable about those things, but she had some gorgeous pieces."

Mrs. Russo's ears perked up and she leaned closer toward Mrs. Grover. "We were just talking about Back Bay Village. They're having a fundraiser, and we're looking for donations of vintage clothes, jewelry and the like. They want to do a fashion show and call it 'Bold, not Old'. What do you think?"

Mrs. Grover gripped her sweater and buttoned it tightly at the top. She pursed her lips and looked down at her plate. "Those people over there are pretty racy. Don't they do that naked polar bear swim? I heard about that somewhere."

Carrie snickered as Mrs. Grover's voice trailed off. "I think there's a small group who does. At least it's in the paper every year. But it's hardly much of a risk here in California. It's not even really that cold on New Year's Day."

"I wasn't referring to the risk to their health. It's just —they're naked."

Jen and Mrs. Russo share a glance and a grin. "Well, the fashion show will not include a polar bear dip. It's going to be closer to Halloween, and I promise you, everyone will have their clothes on. Vintage clothes, even."

The color returned to Mrs. Grover's cheeks as they

ate and chatted about what it used to be like in Newport. She and Mrs. Russo even shared a laugh or two about when they'd first moved there, and how quiet it had been.

Jen knew they were right that it was very different than it had been when she'd grown up there, and she and Joe shared some memories of their own.

"Remember when we could surf or sail all day long, and our parents didn't even look for us until the sun was setting and it was time for dinner?"

"And we'd swim across the bay with no chance of getting hit by a yacht—or a gondola?" Joe added with a smile.

Carrie cleared the dishes when they were finished, and Joe stood and reached into his back pocket for his apron. "I'm ready for dishes," he said as he shooed all the ladies out of the kitchen and into the living room. "You all go talk clothes. I'll bring coffee."

"And bring some of those wedding cookies too, Joey. I made them for Jen, you know."

Jen appreciated Mrs. Russo's thoughtfulness, but couldn't help but smile when she caught Carrie's glance and smirk. "Ooh-la-la," she mouthed as she wiggled her eyebrows.

Jen rolled her eyes and set about showing Mrs. Russo the clothes she'd pulled from Nana's closet.

"I remember that dress," Mrs. Grover said. "It was one of her favorites." She picked it up and held it in front of her, the emerald green sequins sparkling in the lamplight. "Look at these designer labels. Had to have been from the fifties, at least."

"Wow. She was a snappy dresser," Carrie said. "And a petite one, at that."

Mrs. Grover nodded. "Your Nana was really tiny when she was younger. I don't think it'd fit any of us."

"Hm. It certainly wouldn't fit me, that's for sure," Mrs. Russo said, holding another dress in front of her and laughing. "We'll need a wide variety of models to pull this off, it seems. We have to have these in the show. They're gorgeous."

Jen pulled out a Hermes scarf and tied it over her hair again, matching it with a beaded handbag of Nana's.

"You look like Audrey Hepburn," Mrs. Grover and Mrs. Russo said in tandem.

"That's what I said," Joe said from the kitchen.

Mrs. Russo's eyes twinkled. "Oh, Jen, you have to be in the show. You, too, Carrie. It'll be so much fun." She turned to Mrs. Grover. "What about you, Caroline? You game?"

Mrs. Grover twisted her fingers and looked from Carrie to Mrs. Russo to Jen, who all looked at her expectantly.

She looked down at the pile of scarves. "Oh, I don't know. I don't get out much."

"Well, you used to or you wouldn't have so much jewelry, and I've seen you wear it back in the day. It'll be good for you, Caroline. Strap on your dancing shoes. Just say yes," Mrs. Russo said with a kind smile at Mrs. Grover.

Mrs. Grover looked down at her shoes—black and clunky—and over toward Mrs. Russo's strappy sandals, and seemed to make a decision. Still with a bit of hesitation in her eyes, she shook her head slowly but said, "No, I can't."

"Think it over, Mrs. Grover," Joe said as he folded his apron and put it back in his pocket. He brought out a tray of full coffee mugs and pitcher of cream with a bowl of sugar. "Who knows? You may have the time of your life."

Jen waved goodbye to Mrs. Grover, Carrie and Mrs. Russo—but not before Mrs. Russo told her it was one of the best pot roasts she'd ever tasted.

Joe hung back for a moment, and as they turned the corner, Joe whispered, "She doesn't ever say that unless she really means it."

"Well, then, it's an extra special compliment," and she was a little proud of Nana for her recipe holding its own against one of the best cooks Jen could think of.

"Thanks for doing the dishes."

"You're welcome. It's one of my best skills," he said with a broad smile. He gave Jen a kiss on the cheek and squeezed her hand before he walked off to catch up with the others.

Jen blushed when she saw Mrs. Grover's curtain drop and couldn't figure out quite why. What was the harm with a peck on the cheek from an old friend?

She decided that Mrs. Grover just didn't have enough to do, and she headed back up the porch steps, glad that everyone seemed to have a nice time.

TWENTY-ONE

Jen's living room and guest room looked like bombs had gone off in them—but at least Carrie's condo was clean and ready for Bethany's impending arrival. Jen had spent a good part of the week over there cleaning out boxes and getting things in order. Carrie was right. It was all white. White everything—which still seemed strange to Jen as Carrie was such a colorful dresser. She planned to ask Faith later if maybe she had some pillows they could at least put on the white bed for when Bethany arrived.

It had been a lot of work, but they were ready. And now they were looking forward to a relaxing happy hour on Jen's deck. Jen couldn't think of anything she needed more at the moment.

Carrie was even more excited now than when she'd

first heard, and didn't even seem to be bothered that Rob was still furious. He'd relented, but Jen was sure he was still holding a grudge. If he wasn't, Cassidy sure was.

Her phone buzzed, and she checked her texts. Faith was on her way and would be arriving soon, so she hustled up on the appetizer she was trying.

Faith had mentioned that Jen's dad asked her to stop by to pick up some avocados, and Jen realized she hadn't talked to her father in quite some time—not since they'd all agreed to keep the beach house in the family. She made another mental note to call him over the weekend, but was glad that he'd asked Faith to stop by. She'd be happy to get the avocados.

Since she hadn't had any in a while, she'd decided just to make bruschetta and add the avocados. She'd gotten some fresh mozzarella and a baguette at the market, and picked up a basil plant that she thought maybe she could keep alive in her window sill. She'd just finished the balsamic reduction and slicing the tomatoes when Faith and Carrie arrived at the same time.

"Oh, man. Nothing like a real one. Not the grocery store kind," Faith said, sniffing one of the tomatoes. "Nice job."

Jen smiled and certainly agreed. "They'll be perfect with the avocados. Thanks for picking them up."

"No problem." Faith set down a five-gallon bucket

full to the brim. "He said good luck, but they're all going to go bad if he keeps them. Maybe we can give them away to neighbors or something."

"I'll take as many as you want to give me," Carrie said. "Good thing Bethany likes avocados. I don't have much else to offer."

Jen tapped her foot against an ice chest that sat next to the door. "I went shopping for you today. I also made a few things you can heat up over the week while you get your bearings."

"Oh, bless you." Carrie opened the lid and peeked in. She let out a long whistle at the sight of the bread, casseroles, yogurt, milk and loads of vegetables for salad. "Wow, Jen, thanks. We definitely won't starve."

Jen was very happy to help set her friend up. Carrie and Bethany would have enough to worry about besides Carrie's inability to cook. Hopefully, this would start them out.

"And you can come here for dinner any time you want. You know that."

"Man, am I lucky," Carrie said just before the cork gave up its hold on their bottle of wine.

Jen finished putting the bruschetta together, grabbed the platter and followed h er friends out onto the deck.

Faith filled them in on her first week at school. "We

have the usual crowd," she said. "After all these years, it seems like they're blending together a little."

"What do you mean?" Jen drizzled some of the balsamic reduction onto her bruschetta and glanced in Faith's direction.

"Well, there's the class clown. The wriggly kid who won't sit down, no matter what I do. The smart girl who answers all the questions. The shy kid who sits in the corner and wants his mom. They're cute, though. And the first week of kindergarten is always about just establishing order so that you can hope to teach them something."

"I can imagine," Jen said, passing the platter over to Faith. "I remember when Michael walked into kindergarten. He made a friend, and they started talking, walked inside and never looked back."

Faith laughed. "It's just as hard for the parents, you're right. If the school would let them, they'd have their noses pressed to the windows, I'm sure."

Carrie filled their wine glasses up again and took a bruschetta. "Bethany was excited to go to school. She's always liked it. And she liked telling me about what she did all day, too."

Jen's eyebrows rose. "Maybe it's different with girls. When I asked either of the boys how school was, they both said the same thing. 'Fine'. Couldn't get a word out of them unless somebody had brought in a reptile for show and tell."

Carrie laughed. "Maybe girls are different. But Bethany always told me what was going on. I'm looking forward to it."

Jen and Faith shared a quick glance. "Was Maggy like that?" Jen asked.

"Oh, heck no. She clammed up from the time she was fourteen until she was about sixteen, I think. It was tough. Fortunately, nothing nefarious was going on, but we had our moments."

Carrie looked out at the waves. "Yeah, I guess all kids are different."

As excited as Carrie was about this turn of events, it had been a really long time since she'd spent any amount of time with Bethany.

"What if she's—what if she hates me?"

Jen stopped and turned to Carrie. "That's not possible."

"Aw, come on. Anything's possible. It's not as if it's been all chocolate and roses for the past few years. She wouldn't even agree to see me on her sweet sixteenth, remember?"

"Yes, I remember vividly. The three of us decorated the door of the garage with balloons and a 'Happy Sweet

Sixteen, Bethany' in the middle of the night. We're lucky we didn't set the alarms off."

"Yeah, I'm not sure exactly how we got away with that. But she never knew it was me, anyway. She thinks I didn't care."

"Well, she'll know different soon enough," Jen said. "Her room is all ready, and I thought maybe tomorrow the three of us could go shopping for some things to decorate."

"Darn it. Count me out. I have to work at the shop," Faith said. "But I'll be home at night to see what you've come up with, and I left my sewing machines here."

Carrie's phone buzzed, and her eyebrows rose when she looked at the caller ID. "It's Rob," she said, and she stepped inside to take the call.

"You think this is going to be okay?" Faith whispered to Jen when Carrie was inside.

"Sure. I mean, it'll be a big adjustment for Carrie and Bethany, but I think it's a great opportunity. And we're here to help."

Jen stood as Carrie walked slowly back out onto the deck, her face pale.

"What is it? What happened?" Faith stood and crossed the deck, taking Carrie's hand.

"She's not coming. Rob said she changed her mind."

TWENTY-TWO

All the air had been sucked out of Friday night happy hour for Carrie after Rob's call. He hadn't said much more than Bethany had changed her mind—not why, or any other explanation, but he wasn't happy about it, from what she could tell. Apparently, the producers of the show had decided it was better if Bethany didn't go, that they'd focus more on Rob and Cassidy having a second honeymoon, so now a teenager wasn't welcome.

He'd banked on Carrie's offer to take Bethany, and was furious that she was objecting. The whole thing had been crazy-making—at first Rob had been furious that Bethany was *not* going to Europe. It had given Carrie a bit of whiplash, but she still would prefer that Bethany was coming to stay.

"Are you going to try to change her mind?" Jen had asked before Carrie headed home.

The thought had crossed Carrie's mind, but she decided against it. "No, I don't think so. I gave it my best shot the first time. I think at this point, I just need to respect her wishes. Don't you?"

Faith nodded. "Yes, I do. I know it's hard, Carrie. We were all looking forward to spending time with her. But I learned with Maggy that one of worst things I could do was not respect her decisions. Or her boundaries, I should say. If she doesn't want to come, that's just the way it is."

Those words had rung in her ears on her walk home. They rang in her ears as she undressed and took a shower. And they rang in her ears once more as she crawled into bed, the stars just beginning to appear in the evening sky.

Banging on her door woke her up. She wasn't sure what time she'd finally fallen asleep, but it couldn't have been that long ago by the way she felt. She got up, threw on her robe and shuffled downstairs, eyeing her coffee maker on the way to the door.

Whoever was banging on the door hadn't let up, and Carrie swung it open. Jen and Daisy stood on her stoop, and Jen carried a paper bag and a to-go cup. Carrie immediately hoped it was coffee, and she managed a smile when Jen held out the cup to her.

"I've been texting you all morning. Did you just get up?"

Carrie nodded, about all she could do until the caffeine hit her veins. She was normally a morning person, but her first order of business was always coffee.

"Thank you. I needed this."

Jen came in and closed the door behind her. "I figured. How are you doing?"

Carrie shrugged. "I have no idea. I've only been awake for a minute. Didn't sleep very well."

"To be expected. I thought maybe it would be good for you to get outside. Daisy and I are walking to Dory's by the pier to get some fish for Sunday dinner tomorrow. Want to go?"

"Uh, I don't know. Not feeling very peppy, to be honest. Faith wouldn't go with you?"

"She had to go to work at the shop. She's really burning the candle at both ends. But no, she couldn't go."

"I don't know. I'm not in a great mood."

Jen opened the bag and set two muffins on a paper towel. "Might this help?" she asked, nudging a muffin in Carrie's direction. "Your favorite. Blueberry."

Carrie ran her hand through her hair. "Those are Bethany's favorite, too."

"Yeah. I know. I made them for her. There are some in the ice chest I packed for you. I can bring it over later. You might as well have something to eat. You left last night without it."

"I'm sorry. I just wasn't—I needed to just come home."

Jen stood when Daisy tugged at her leash, her nose stuck in the crack of the door. "Right. But enough of that. Let's go blow the cobwebs out. A walk'll do you some good. And I haven't been to the fish market in a while. I bet they'll have some different stuff. Hoping they have some yellow tail or red snapper."

"Yum. I'll grill it tomorrow night if they do."

Jen opened the door and smiled. "I was counting on it. Hurry up and get dressed and I'll meet you on the boardwalk. Daisy's got absolutely no patience at all."

Carrie finished her coffee, splashed some water on her face and threw on some clothes. As she passed by Bethany's bedroom—her spare room—she sighed and closed the door on her dreams, not daring to hope that things might get better.

TWENTY-THREE

Jen had given up trying to get Carrie out of the house for the rest of the weekend. She'd seemed like she was doing all right—Carrie had a unique ability to bounce back from disappointment. She sure had quite a lot of practice, thanks to her mother.

"Need any help?" Faith asked as she came down the narrow stairs from her room. She'd clearly just taken a shower, and even though she should be exhausted, she looked bright and perky. Her dark hair was still damp, but fell around her face in the waves that were so pretty on both her and Maggy.

"You look nice," Jen said with a smile.

Faith's eyebrows rose and she looked down at her faded jeans, t-shirt and flip flops. "Wow, you're easy to impress."

Jen laughed and handed Faith a roll of aluminum. "You look happy, maybe I should have said."

"Thanks. I am." Faith eyed the red snapper, the fingerling potatoes and asparagus that Jen had seasoned earlier.

"How many?" Faith asked. They'd cooked together for so many years that she knew exactly what Jen was making—snapper in foil packets on the grill.

"I think eight should be enough. Maggy's not coming up, right?"

"No, not tonight."

"Okay. Then there won't be that many of us. Michael and Amber can't make it either."

"Maybe next weekend," Faith replied. She tore off eight pieces of foil and as Jen added the seasoned fish, some asparagus, potatoes and butter to each packet, she folded them up and set them on a platter.

"When's Carrie going to be here?" Faith said when they were finished.

"Any minute, I think. I tried to get her to go walking again today while you were at the shop, but she didn't want to. She wasn't too bad, though. Didn't want to talk about anything. I tried."

Faith shook her head. "I don't know how she does it. I guess years of experience with her mom and—well, just life. She handles disappointment better than anybody I know."

Jen handed Faith a corkscrew and gestured to the refrigerator, where she'd chilled the chardonnay for dinner.

Faith narrowed her eyes as she opened the bottle of wine. "Her mom is really awful. Why is she like that? Why has she always been like that?"

"I've wondered myself. Carrie's so—I don't know. She's so nice. A great dentist. Never been in real trouble. She was an easy kid, mostly. I mean, we did minor stuff when we were kids but nothing big. But her mom really wasn't around much. She was always at a party or fundraiser with her dad."

"Maybe some moms just are a little distant. I have a co-worker whose mom is always finding stuff wrong with her, too. She says she just chalks it up to that's the kind of mom she got."

Jen took the glass of wine Faith held out and nodded. "Maybe some moms are just a little self-absorbed. I don't know. But I can't imagine doing to my kids what Mrs. Westland does to Carrie. I just can't."

Faith picked up the bowl of guacamole Jen had made earlier and followed her friend out onto the deck. "Neither can I. I mean, a lot of moms aren't all that close with their kids, but it's something else completely to sabotage them, over and over."

"Agreed. And unfortunately, we may never know."

Jen set the bowl of chips on the table outside and settled into one of the deck chairs. "Ah, what a nice evening."

"It sure is," Carrie said as she came through the deck, giving Daisy a pat and setting the bottle of wine she'd brought on the table.

Faith handed her a glass of wine and found her favorite deck chair. "How are you doing?" she asked Carrie.

Carrie took a sip of her wine and smiled. "Lovely weather we're having."

Jen rolled her eyes. "Oh, it's going to be one of those nights, eh?"

Carrie laughed. "I'm all talked out. I'm thought out. I'm just moving on."

Jen sighed. She could tell Carrie had reached her limit, and she respected that. There really wasn't that much to say anymore.

"How's it going with the clothes for the fashion show? Found anything cool?" Faith asked, willing to change the subject also.

"Oh, let me show you one of the things I found. It's so weird—Nana was a pretty practical dresser, as far as I knew. But she sure had a different life before I came along. Seems like these fancy dresses from the fifties were pretty expensive, too."

She rushed into the house and grabbed the dress she'd found earlier.

"Check this out," she said as she held it in front of her.

Faith whistled and stood, unable to resist running her fingers over the satin skirt that poofed out at the bottom with what must have been a crinoline layer underneath.

"Wow. And look at that beading. It's gorgeous."

The dress had a scoop neck with small capped sleeves that fell off the shoulder. The bodice was beaded with thousands of black sparkles. It cinched tight at the waist and in the front rested a satin bow.

"Gosh. That looks like something that would be in a movie, not in your Nana's closet."

Jen nodded. "I thought the same thing. Who knew she had so many fancy things. And there's a clutch to match."

"Maybe Mrs. Russo or Mrs. Grover remember where she might have worn something like that. They've been around forever, too."

"Well, I wouldn't say forever," Mrs. Grover said as

she leaned over the fence between the two houses. She laughed and nodded. "I remember that dress, though."

"You do? Well, come on over and tell us about it."

Mrs. Grover did just that. She explained that long ago, when Newport was still growing, there were all kinds of celebrity events and grand openings. There weren't as many people, so most of the locals knew each other.

"Your grandmother used to love to go to those things. And she was so lovely, inside and out, that she got lots of invitations. I think she wore that one to the grand opening of Fashion Island. It was quite an event."

"Wow," Jen said. "When was that?"

"I think around '67, but don't quote me."

"How fun that was, I bet." Jen twirled around, and the dress spun perfectly.

"Not if you ask me," Carrie said. "My mom used to drag me to all of those things when I was little. They were awful."

"Maybe for a kid, but I don't know. The fundraiser was fun. We don't do that kind of stuff very often."

"Yes, and with good reason. My mom gave up even inviting me years ago," Carrie said.

Jen and Faith exchanged a quick glance, and Jen thought maybe that's why it was so odd with Carrie and her mother. They really were like night and day.

Just as Carrie said, "I'd better light the barbecue," her phone buzzed in her pocket.

"Good grief," she said before she walked out onto the sidewalk to answer. She couldn't have been on the phone more than a minute before she hung up, closed her eyes and pinched the bridge of her nose.

"What?" Jen asked, leaning against the deck railing.

Carrie sighed. "Apparently, there's been a change of plans again. Rob's waiting at my house. With Bethany. And her luggage."

Jen stood and glanced at Faith. "You want me to go with you?"

"No. I'm good," Carrie said. "Sorry about the barbecue."

Jen shook her head. "No problem. Just go, and call me later."

Carrie nodded started home, walking faster than Jen had seen her do in a long time.

Mrs. Grover twisted her fingers as they all three watched Carrie round the corner. "I certainly hope everything's all right. Carrie's such a dear."

Jen nodded. "She's been through enough lately. She doesn't need any more trouble."

TWENTY-FOUR

If Carrie thought she had whiplash the other day, she was pretty positive she did now. She couldn't keep up with all this, and she wondered what had caused the current change of events as she walked home as fast as she could, even jogging a little.

She rounded the corner to her house and stopped in her tracks. A black limo sat outside her front door, and Rob and Bethany stood on the sidewalk. He yelled as he shook his finger at her, and she stood as far away from him as she could, her arms folded.

Bethany's frown was more confirmation for Carrie that this was not a good thing. At least not something that was going well. It didn't look at all like Bethany had changed her mind or was there willingly. That's not something Carrie had anticipated, even for one second.

"Hi," she said as she approached, and both Bethany and Rob stopped talking and looked at the ground.

"Hi," Rob said, taking a searing glance at Bethany. "I hope your offer still stands. We've got to get to the airport, and Bethany has decided she'd be thrilled to stay with you. Haven't you, Bethany?"

Bethany glanced up at her father, and Carrie thought if looks could kill, he'd be dead by now.

"Right," she said, and looked back down at her shoes.

"Where should I put these bags, sir?" the limo driver asked.

"Um, I guess right inside the door," Carrie said with a shrug. "Bethany, why don't you go wait inside. The door's open. I want to talk to your dad for a minute."

Bethany grabbed her tennis rackets and slung them over her shoulder. She turned so fast that her ponytail flittered across Rob's face and he glared after her. "Thanks. Goodbye to you, too. Yes, we'll have a wonderful time. Thank you."

Bethany slammed the door and Carrie blinked after her a few times before turning to Rob.

"What's that all about? She doesn't seem thrilled to me. Not by a long shot."

"Sure she is. She just needs to adjust," Rob said, still looking at the front door.

Carrie didn't believe him for one second, but she

didn't quite know what to do. "I'm not sure she should stay here if she doesn't want to. Things are strained enough."

The tinted window in the back of the limo rolled down, and Cassidy poked her white-blonde head out.

"Hurry up, honey. We need to get going. We're going to be late for our flight."

Carrie summoned every ounce of manners she could and said, "Hello, Cassidy. I hope you have a nice trip."

Cassidy looked up, her hand shielding her eyes from the sun, and seemed to notice Carrie for the first time.

"Oh, hello. Thank you. I'm sure it will be lovely. A second honeymoon, after all," she said, her blue eyes cold. She flipped her hair and poured herself a glass of champagne, then gave Carrie a nod and a very fake smile, rolling the window back up again.

"I have to go. She won't be a problem. She's mostly at school and tennis, and then tournaments on the week-end. Armand, here, will take care of transportation." He gestured at the tall man standing at the back of the limo, and he gave Carrie a nod and a more sincere smile than Cassidy had. "Just feed her and keep her alive, if you can. I don't expect any more than that."

Carrie couldn't for the life of her understand why he'd put up such fuss about keeping Bethany with him if this was how he treated her. It made her blood boil, and if she could have slapped him without making a scene, she would have.

Cassidy rolled down the window again and glared at Rob. "If we miss this flight, I will never forgive you," she said with a big pout on her face. She sounded just like she did on the one TV episode Carrie had been able to stomach, and Rob was equally gross.

"I'm sorry, kitten. I'm coming." He turned to Carrie and held out a fat envelope. "This should take care of everything else," he said.

"I don't want that," she said, holding her palms out toward him. "I don't need it." She hadn't expected him to give her a wad of cash, and that wouldn't have made her feel very good about being with her daughter. It felt more like a babysitter, and she'd been looking forward to just spending time with Bethany, not making any money.

"Suit yourself," he said, stuffing the envelope in the inside pocket of his suit and crossing to the other wide of the limo.

Armand nodded at Carrie again and opened the door for Rob, and he slid in beside Cassidy. She handed him a glass of champagne and turned back to Carrie one last time with what could only be described as a smirk on her face. "Thanks for the vacation from that," she said, jutting her chin toward the front door. "It'll be nice to have a break. And good luck."

The window rolled up again and all Carrie could see was black as it pulled away and turned onto Newport Boulevard.

She stood on the sidewalk for a minute or two, grappling with the obvious—that things weren't exactly as she'd thought they were in Bethany's world. She turned toward the door, knowing that she needed to find out more and hoping she could help.

TWENTY-FIVE

Bethany sat on the couch, her phone in her hand.

"So, I'm pretty sure that the story your dad gave isn't the real one, is it?" Carrie asked, leaning forward, her elbows on her knees.

Bethany didn't bother to look up from her phone when she answered.

"If you want to know the truth, I really didn't want to come here. I haven't talked to you for years. I don't really know you. Kind of awkward, don't you think?"

Carrie suddenly realized that she might have been a little naive to think that it would all be hunky-dory if Bethany were to stay. She'd been so wrapped up in her excitement that she'd barely paid attention when people said, "Be careful what you wish for." But just because

Bethany wanted to be somewhere else didn't mean that they couldn't get along, give it a good try.

"Actually, I was hoping we could use this opportunity to get to know each other again."

"Look, I just need a place to crash for a month. I appreciate you letting me do it here. I won't even be here very much, so I'll try not to bother you. I know it's annoying to have kids around."

She stood and rolled her suitcases to the bottom of the stairs and grabbed her tennis rackets.

This wasn't going particularly well, Carrie thought, but she was pretty sure that she shouldn't push the envelope. She'd never once said kids were annoying to have around—that sounded more like something her own mother would say. But not her.

"I'm very happy to have you here," she said. "Very."

"Great," Bethany said, looking up the staircase. "Can you tell me where to crash? I have homework I have to do for tomorrow."

Carrie stood and grabbed one of the suitcases. "Sure, follow me."

She set Bethany's suitcase on the bed and opened the sliding glass door to the small balcony. "I hope it's okay. You've got your own bathroom, through there. Sorry it's not decorated more. I never got around to it. We could paint it if you like. You can pick the colors."

Bethany shrugged, then put her other suitcase on the bed. "Nah. I'm not going to be here that long."

Carrie fiddled with the hem of her shirt and looked around the room. It really was just white. She'd meant to get those pillows from Faith but hadn't when she thought Bethany wasn't coming.

"Okay. The dresser is empty," she said, pointing to the antique walnut dresser on the other side of the room. There was also a matching vanity—both antiques that Carrie had had when she was a little girl. "Feel free to make yourself at home."

Bethany looked around the room for a minute. She took the suitcases, set them against the wall on the floor and unzipped them. "I won't need that. Like I said, I won't be here very long."

Carrie found herself blinking several times, her eyebrows raised. She didn't quite know what to say, and decided not to push.

"Suit yourself. You hungry? I can make you something to eat."

"You can?" Bethany asked. "If I remember correctly, you don't know how to cook."

Carrie thought she may as well laugh about that because it was true, and she did. "Yes, well, some things haven't changed. Jen loaded up the fridge for us when I thought you were coming. But I do know how to get takeout."

"Right," Bethany said as she hung up what looked like tennis outfits in the closet.

She opened her backpack and plopped some big textbooks on the bed.

"Would you prefer to study downstairs? I didn't think to put a desk in here."

Bethany shook her head. "No, thanks. I'm good. I do need to get this done, though."

"Oh, right. Okay. Well, help yourself to anything at all. I guess I don't need to take you to school? I thought I would be doing that."

"No, Armand's got it. It's covered."

Carrie nodded. "Okay. I put shampoo, soap, a razor and other stuff in the bathroom for you. Fresh towels, too. Do you need me to wake you up for school?" Carrie had very fond memories of waking Bethany up when she was little, usually with a, "Rise and shine!"

Bethany looked at Carrie like she'd just said the dumbest thing ever known to man. "I'm sixteen. No, I don't need you to wake me up for school."

"Okay. Got it. Well, let me know if you need anything."

Bethany was already flipping through the pages of

her biology book, pencil in hand. "Sure. Thanks. And can you close the door on your way out?"

TWENTY-SIX

Carrie closed her bedroom door behind her and dialed Jen.

"I've been dying to hear what's going on," Jen said when she picked up.

"Not much," Carrie responded. She put her phone on speaker and set it down in the bathroom, changing into her comfy clothes—sweats and a t-shirt—while she was talking.

"Rob dropped her off in a limo. She's in her room doing homework. Doesn't want dinner. End of story."

"What do you mean, end of story? Did she change her mind again and decide to stay with you?"

Carrie smoothed some moisturizer over her face and reached for a headband to tie her hair back.

"Sort of. Well, not really, I guess. I think there was nowhere else for her to stay. Pretty sure he forced her."

She picked up the phone again and took it off speaker, sliding her feet into her comfy slippers.

"Oh. So she's there as an unwilling guest."

"Pretty much," Carrie said, plopping down onto her bed.

"Is she being rude?"

Carrie shook her head, even though Jen couldn't see her. "No, not really. She said thanks. She just doesn't want to have much to do with me. And doesn't want to eat. Said she has homework and asked me to close the door."

Jen paused for a moment. "Well, I'm sure she does have homework. Try not to take it personally."

"I'm trying. But I think she should eat something, don't you?"

"I know she's got a little bit of history not wanting to eat, but she looks healthy, right? Just pay attention. Set something out for her. Maybe one of the muffins, or something. My experience with teenagers is that they'll eat when they're hungry."

"Yeah, but you had boys. They'll eat no matter what."

Jen laughed. "True. But don't have your pain in advance. Just pay attention. It could be nothing. This is a big change for her, too. You going to take her to school in the morning?"

Carrie headed out into the kitchen and looked in the fridge. She'd missed dinner, too.

"No. Can you believe they've got a limo taking her, to and from? Jeez."

"Oh, wow."

"I'm sure Cassidy likes the attention, even once removed. I would hate that, but Bethany didn't seem to mind."

"She doesn't have her driver's license? I'm surprised he hasn't bought her a car like all the other rich parents."

Carrie chuckled. "I guess not. Remember that old Volkswagen my dad got me when I turned sixteen so I could drive to school? That old beat up one that he had painted orange?"

Carrie could picture Jen snickering on the other end.

"Yep. But hey, we had lots of fun in that old bug. Took it to Mexico more than once for shrimp and lobster."

"Right. I don't know that I'd do that in a limo."

"No. Well, you sound all right."

Carrie pulled some of Jen's lasagna out of the fridge. "I am. And thanks for the food. At least if she starves, it'll have been her choice, not my inability to cook."

"You're welcome. I also put in a bag of granola bars.

She can take some to school if she wants, but I bet she buys lunch there."

"Probably," Carrie said as she put the plate of lasagna she'd cut into the microwave. "Sorry I had to leave before the barbecue. And that I couldn't grill the snapper."

"No problem at all. Turns out Mrs. Grover is a pretty good back-up for you. I saved you some. I'll put it in your fridge tomorrow while you're at work."

Carrie thanked her friend and signed off, but not before saying, "Tell Faith I'm sorry I didn't get to see her much, and have a good week at work. Everything good with her?"

Jen paused for a moment. "She's okay. She's got a lot going on, but she likes working at the shop. She said the owner gave her a key, and won't be there next weekend. Kind of weird, but Faith's excited."

"Oh, good," Carrie said. "Talk to you tomorrow."

"Okay. And Carrie, try not to worry. It's going to be fine. It's only a month anyway. It'll fly by."

Not for the first time, she wondered what she'd do without her friends—she'd be a mess.

She heated up the lasagna and her stomach grumbled. The garlic bread Jen sent smelled fantastic, and she set a piece of it on her plate. Just as she sat at the kitchen island, she heard Bethany's bedroom door open, and her feet pad down the stairs.

"Hi," she said as she leaned against the kitchen island. "I guess I am hungry, and that smells good. Jen's lasagna? I haven't had that in a long time."

Carrie smiled and nudged the plate toward Bethany. "Yep. Help yourself."

Bethany shifted from one foot to the other, and looked from the lasagna to Jen and back. "Thanks. Mind if I take it up in my room? I'm still doing homework."

Carrie wished that she would sit down at the island and talk to her a bit more, but at least she wanted to eat. That was probably all she could hope for at the moment, so she nodded and handed her a napkin.

"There's milk in the fridge and some other drinks. Help yourself."

Bethany nodded, and pulled a juice box out of. She smiled at Carrie—well, it wasn't really a smile, but it wasn't a frown, either—and headed upstairs with her dinner.

Carrie leaned on the island, her chin resting on her hand. It wasn't exactly the family reunion she'd hoped for, but at least she didn't have to worry about Bethany being anorexic. She could cross that off her list. Now, all she had to worry about were the thousand other things that could go wrong.

TWENTY-SEVEN

Friday night happy hour came quickly, and Jen had invited Mrs. Russo and Mrs. Grover tonight. Joe was working, piloting gondolas as someone had called out sick, and Faith had just arrived. When Mrs. Russo, Mrs. Grover and Carrie got there, they headed in to look at all the fantastic things Jen had found during the week.

Mrs. Russo laughed with gusto when she held up the beautiful, little black dress of Nana's and looked at herself in the mirror.

"I think only my right side would fit in this. I'd need another entire dress for my left side."

"Oh, that's not true," Mrs. Grover said, and Jen, Carrie and Faith all looked at her since it may have been a little true. Mrs. Russo wasn't especially big—the dress was especially small.

Mrs. Grover blushed. "Well, maybe not two whole dresses," she said, trying to backpedal best she could. "It's a tiny dress. It wouldn't fit any of us."

Mrs. Russo set the dress back down on the bed in one of Jen's guest rooms. "Right. But a lot of this other stuff would fit all of us." She stole a peek out of the corner of her eye at Carrie and Faith. "Don't you think?" Jen picked up a pink cotton gingham sleeveless blouse with buttons up the back. "This is cute."

"And it would look great on you," Mrs. Russo said, her eyebrows wiggling. "Maybe with some white capris?"

"I'm sure all of these things would look great on the models," Jen said as she separated the scarves from the dresses and the pants. "These slim pants you all wore were so flattering. Kind of like capris, but so much cuter. Right at the ankle."

"I'm not sure about those. Some of this stuff looks weird to me," Carrie said, holding up a black sequined sweater.

Faith and Jen laughed out loud. "Good thing you're not in charge of this fundraiser. With your fashion sense, it's a blessing for all of us."

"What?" Carrie said, looking down at her white dress with aqua, orange and yellow flowers on it. Her matching yellow sandals—well, at least they matched.

"Some of this stuff is so cute, I'd wear it now," Faith said. "So how does this work. Are you going to sell the clothes?"

"The way it was explained to me is that ladies will model the clothes, people bid on them and the proceeds go to the village—in this case, their bridge club. All the money made in the bridge club goes to the local Boys' and Girls' Club."

Mrs. Grover pulled a face. "That was your Nana's favorite bridge club. I never went because they were a little—well, you know. Racy."

Carrie frowned. "How can a bridge club be racy?"

"Well, they serve cocktails. In the daytime. At noon."

"I'm sure they weren't the only ones," Mrs. Russo added. "Anyway, I do know it was one of your grand-mother's favorite clubs. So thanks for being willing to donate."

"Sure," Jen said. "But if you guys want any of this stuff beforehand, just let me know."

Faith came out of the bathroom and everybody gasped. She looked stunning—her dark hair really stood out against the soft color.

"Oh, my gosh, that looks perfect on you," Carrie gushed.

And she was right. Jen zipped up the back of the dress and turned Faith around in front of the mirror. Their eyes met, and Jen smiled when Faith's eyes grew wide. Since her divorce, Faith had worn mostly jeans and t-shirts—and little fancier ones for teaching, but jeans and t-shirts nonetheless. It was nice to see her in a fancy dress, as she was beautiful.

"It sure does," Mrs. Russo added. "These clothes are perfect for you girls."

"They really are fun to wear. The ladies at the village will have a blast in them."

"Uh, well, that's the thing." Mrs. Russo looked down and ran the hem of one of the dresses between her fingers."

"What's the thing?" Carrie asked.

Mrs. Russo looked at all the women in turn, and then back down at the dress. "I knew these would look great on you guys. And Phyllis said that nobody at the village wanted to model, they were more anxious to sit in the audience, have a good lunch and bid on the clothes."

Jen leaned against the dresser, her arms folded as she looked at Mrs. Russo and smiled.

The older woman looked like she was about to confess that she'd taken the last cookie out of the cookie jar. "I may have told my friend Phyllis that we would model."

"We? We who?" Faith asked as she smoothed the satin of her dress.

"All of us," Mrs. Russo said, looking around the room.

They all exchanged glances, and Jen noticed that everyone was smiling—except Mrs. Grover.

Her hand tightened on the tip button of her cardigan. "I couldn't possibly."

"That's fine, Caroline, although I think it would be good for you." Mrs. Russo turned to Jen. "What do you guys say? You in for a little fun? Free lunch, raising money for a good cause?"

Faith said as she wriggled out of the gorgeous dress. "When is it?"

"Not for three weeks. We have plenty of time to see who should wear what."

Jen shrugged. "I'm in. That'll give me time to go through the rest of the closets in the house, see what's what. And if it was Nana's favorite bridge club, it's perfect."

"I guess it's okay with me," Carrie said. "Bethany's here, but all she does is go to school, play tennis tournaments and do her homework. She won't even know if I'm gone."

"Aw, that's sad. You guys really haven't had a chance to talk or anything?" Jen asked.

"Nope. She has been eating, though. Your lasagna

got her started, and she did ask me to thank you for all the food."

"Oh, that's good. Sounds like a typical teenager to me," Jen said, but she caught the wistful look on Carrie's face. She knew Carrie would like more, but at least nothing bad was going on. At the moment.

"Great," Mrs. Russo said when everybody—except Mrs. Grover—had agreed to participate. She picked up the gorgeous little black dress and held it up again. "Now all we need to do is find somebody who can fit in this smaller stuff. I don't think anybody would want to see me in it. Might blind somebody."

TWENTY-EIGHT

Carrie waved as Armand closed the door behind Bethany and hopped in the driver's seat. He seemed like a nice man, and Carrie had learned a little bit more over the past week. He'd picked up Bethany every day for school, and each time he'd brought her a Starbuck's green tea.

One morning while he was waiting, she invited him in and they sat at the island waiting for Bethany. He'd told her that Bethany liked it with honey and lemon, and that she usually made her own with the Keurig in the kitchen. But since she didn't have that, he'd picked one up for her every day.

Carrie ordered one of the machines that very day, with the cups that went with it—green tea for Bethany and coffee for herself, and some hot chocolate—and it should be arriving later that afternoon.

Beyond that, they'd pretty much fended for themselves. Bethany had a tennis tournament, and Carrie had asked if she could come watch. Bethany had hesitated for a moment, but had said no, she'd prefer if Carrie didn't. Carrie did her best to hide her disappointment, but didn't want to push.

Dirk called right after Bethany left, and Carrie couldn't hide her disappointment any longer. "I keep asking her if she needs help, if I can come watch tennis, but she just says no. I don't really know what to do."

Dirk sighed. "I know what you mean. It's taken a lot to get Abby to let me come watch. And even then, it's only sometimes."

"I don't get it. Why wouldn't they want us to come?"

Dirk laughed. "I've come to realize that it's about their wanting to be—well, autonomous, I guess. They have their own world, their own friends. At this age, they're flexing all those muscles. At least she lets me come sometimes. Maybe Bethany will, too."

Carrie realized she was stirring the sugar in the sugar bowl and set the spoon down. "I don't know. She really doesn't want to have anything to do with me. She doesn't seem angry, exactly, just really—guarded, I guess."

"Ah, another classic trait of the teenage species," Dirk said with a laugh. "And we're not the first or the last parents to be frustrated by it, I'm sure. Just give it time."

Carrie smiled. Dirk always made her feel like everything was going to be all right, and she really liked that about him.

"Hey, even if we can't go to the tennis tournament, we can hit some balls around. We said we were going to. I have the day off. How about today?"

Carrie stood and stretched. "I haven't played in years, but I did find my racket when Jen and I were cleaning out the guest room. Sure, that sounds great." She hadn't exercised in a while, either, and it might be good to change that.

"Fantastic. I'm a member at the club by the harbor. How about if I reserve a court at eleven? We can hit a little bit and go to lunch afterward."

"Perfect. I'll meet you there," Carrie said.

She straightened up the house and called Jen in the meantime.

"That sounds fun. You love tennis."

"I do," Carrie responded. "I don't think I can play very well, though. Been a long time."

"You're a natural. Remember, you taught Bethany and she's doing great. A champion."

Carrie glanced over at the box on top of the fridge. She'd kept every newspaper article about Bethany's wins —and losses—over the years, every interview, every award. "Well, she's a lot younger. Wish me luck."

"Better yet, break a leg. Oh, no, wait. The opposite," Jen said with a laugh before they ended the call.

Carrie sifted through her tennis outfits and chose her favorite, a lime green short skirt and matching top. Nobody had been happier than she was when tennis whites didn't matter anymore and tennis attire became much more interesting.

She reached for her rackets, her backpack that held her tennis balls and a bottle of water and headed out the door.

When she got to the club, she spotted Dirk immediately. She cocked her head and looked a little closer. He was tall, and very handsome, if she was honest. He was warming up against a backboard, and she noticed that his swing was clean and strong. He'd probably give her a run for her money.

She wasn't sure if he'd noticed that she'd arrived, as he was pretty intent on practicing his serve. But as she walked up, he said, "Gosh. I've been looking out for you, but I couldn't have missed you, I see. Could see you coming from a mile away. That's definitely a tennis power outfit."

She smiled, and imagined that he was referring to her lime green visor that matched her outfit. It was a little bright.

"Well, good. All the better to beat you, sir."

"Ah, them's fighting words," Dirk said as he picked up his bucket of tennis balls and guided her toward the court he'd reserved.

They played for a couple of hours, and Carrie was pleased that everything came back to her, just like riding a bike. She and Dirk were pretty evenly matched, and they ended up playing two sets, tying at one each.

She happily followed him to the restaurant he'd suggested—Woody's Wharf. It was one of the older restaurants in Newport, and one of her favorites.

Over his burger and her Mahi Mahi sandwich, they laughed about the match, shared about the kids and Dirk again told her to just be patient.

"You know, if you let her have her space, it'll go easier on you. Maybe by the end of her time, we can get the girls to play us in doubles."

"Oh, wow, that'd be so fun. I don't have much hope of that, though. She'll barely speak to me, let alone agree to something like that."

Dirk's eyes twinkled. "Stranger things have happened. Let's just keep practicing, though, just in case."

Carrie laughed and got that feeling again. Dirk made her feel safe, and hopeful. She didn't want to get too confident, but maybe he was right. She crossed her fingers under the table, just for good measure.

TWENTY-NINE

Carrie closed the door slowly behind her. None of her crossed fingers or hopefulness in her heart had prepared her for Bethany's flat-out refusal to go with her to Jen's for Sunday barbecue.

She'd just ignored the silence all week. She'd kept a smile on her face. She'd made sure Bethany had everything she needed. But she really didn't think that Bethany wouldn't want to see Jen and Faith—and even Maggy. But when Carrie had told her she'd be heading over to Jen's beach house at five, and she hoped Bethany would come along, Bethany had just shaken her head.

"Thank Jen for me, but no. I have things I need to do."

She'd just come home from her tennis tournament and needed a shower. Carrie could understand that. But to not come and say hello—these were her lifelong friends as well, after all—was more than Carrie could understand.

"Are you sure? They miss you. They love you, just like I do," had been on the tip of Carrie's tongue, but Jen and Dirk's words rang in her ears. 'Just give her time, and space.'

But it really stung. One week of the four was gone, and at the current pace, by the time Bethany went back with Rob and Cassidy, they would have spoken less than a hundred words between them.

She slung the bag with wine and cheese over her shoulder and set out toward Jen's. She would have stayed home if she'd thought Bethany would do something with her. Or talk to her. Or anything at all. But based on the last week, she'd be in her room with the door closed, coming out only to eat. So Carrie figured she might as well go see her friends. And she was sure Jen was counting on her to barbecue something. At least she was wanted somewhere.

Her phone vibrated in her pocket and she groaned when she saw the caller ID. Her mother was the last person in the world she wanted to talk to. They hadn't spoken since the debacle at the fundraiser, and that had been weeks ago, now.

But she knew from experience that when her mother did start calling, she was relentless.

It was a beautiful evening—the seagulls soared over the beach and the light glinted on the waves as the sun began its descent toward the horizon. As the warm breeze brushed against her cheeks, she decided now was as good a time as any to answer. "Hello, Mother," she said as she walked along the boardwalk.

"Hello, Carrie. How are you?"

Thousands of legitimate angry responses flitted through Carrie's head, but she settled on the usual one.

"Fine. How are you?"

"Just fine, dear. I'll get right to the point. I hear you're involved in another fundraiser, one for the Back Bay Village."

Carrie started to wonder how her mother had heard about that, but realized that her mother knew everything that happened in Newport. Especially when it came to fundraisers.

"Not really. Just modeling in a fashion show. Helping out Mrs. Russo."

"Oh, so Gina Russo has a hand in this."

Carrie frowned. "A hand in it? It's just a fundraiser. It was Jen's grandmother's favorite bridge club. We're just helping out."

"Hm. Well, I've played bridge there also and I'd like to come. Send me a ticket, please."

Carrie stopped in her tracks. It was one thing that her mother hadn't even apologized about inviting Rob and Cassidy to the fundraiser that she and Dirk put together. It was quite another for her to come to another one and attempt to ruin that one, too.

"No, Mother. I don't want you to come. This is Mrs. Russo's and her friends' show. I'm just helping out on the side."

"All the more reason you shouldn't mind if I come. I can bring friends who would be happy to donate."

"No. Thank you, but no."

Her mother paused on the line. "You're not still annoyed about Rob and Cassidy at the hospital fundraiser, are you? He insisted, you know. They are big donors. How could I possibly refuse?"

All of the things Carrie wanted to say ran through her head. "You should have known it would be hard for me. You should have asked me first. You should never have considered it in the first place. And once again, your image was more important than your daughter's feelings."

But she said none of those things. "Please just respect my wishes. For once."

Her mother sputtered something in response, but

Carrie just ended the call and dropped her phone back in her pocket. It vibrated again immediately, but instead of answering, she turned it off.

"Who was that?" Jen asked as she passed through the gate and gave Daisy a pat on the head.

"My mom. She wants to come to the fundraiser at the village. I told her no."

"You did?" Jen said, her eyebrows raised.

"I did. Maybe it'll work."

Faith didn't look too convinced. "Maybe. But at least you said it."

Carrie reached for the bottle of wine and handed it to Faith. "Yeah. For what it's worth."

"Where's Bethany? Maggy will be here any minute," Faith said as she began to open the wine.

Carrie plopped down on one of the deck chairs. "Oof. She's not coming."

"Oh, no," Faith said with a frown. "We were all so excited to see her."

"I know. I was excited, too, to have more than five words pass between us in a week. She said she's tired, and has homework. What she's been saying for a week."

Faith and Jen looked as sad as Carrie felt, but she had no idea what to do about it. Maybe all she was going to be able to do was keep Bethany alive, like Rob said, and that wasn't at all what she'd hoped for.

"You all look awful. Who died?" Maggy, Faith's daughter, asked as she came through the gate and knelt down to pet Daisy.

"Hi, honey. Carrie just said Bethany didn't want to come."

Maggy looked equally disappointed. "Oh, no. I really wanted to see her."

"Same here," Carrie said, and Maggy looked at her for a moment, then smiled.

"I'll be right back," she said, handing her bag to her mother. She headed back through the gate and rounded the corner toward Carrie's house so quickly that nobody had a chance to say anything, but Carrie crossed her fingers again just for luck.

THIRTY

The racks of ribs that Jen had put in the oven a couple of hours earlier smelled delicious, and she had been excited to surprise Bethany. They were one of Bethany's favorites, or at least had been when she'd last seen her. But that had been over four years ago, and she was disappointed that she wouldn't have the chance to see her.

She put the finishing touches on the homemade barbecue sauce for Carrie to brush on them when they went on the grill.

Since Maggy left, they hadn't talked much—mostly had stared at the corner Maggy had disappeared around, waiting for her to come back.

Faith finished her chip—Jen had made Bethany's favorite guacamole just for the occasion—and filled Carrie's wine glass.

"What do you think's happening?" Carrie asked.

Jen stepped back onto the deck, a platter of ribs and bowl of sauce in her hands.

"No telling," she said quietly. She smiled at Carrie. "I'm sure everything's fine. You mind starting the ribs on the grill?"

Carrie took another look toward the boardwalk and sighed. "Sure. No problem. They'll take a bit, though."

"No problem. The cole slaw and corn on the cob are already done. Just have to do the garlic bread at the last minute. Make sure you give me a ten-minute head's up."

"Okay, sure." Carrie took the platter from Jen and headed toward the grill in back of the house.

Jen sat down beside Faith and they exchanged a quick glance. "I sure wish I could help somehow," Jen said.

"Same here, but maybe we'll get a chance after all." Faith stood and pointed toward the corner with a wide smile.

"Oh, my gosh, she came," Jen exclaimed. They both rushed toward the gate and Daisy wagged her tail wildly, even though she didn't know why.

"Carrie," Jen called as she hit the bottom step and held her arms wide toward Bethany. Maggy followed behind, a sly smile on her face.

"We're so glad you're here, sweetheart," Jen said as

she wrapped Bethany in her arms. She didn't want to over-do it, but she was just so happy to see her that she couldn't help herself.

"Aw, so nice of you to come," Faith said as she got her turn for a hug.

Bethany turned and smiled shyly at Maggy. "I wouldn't have, but I got to take a shower and Maggy came over. It's been a long time. It's really good to see you guys."

Jen grabbed Bethany's hand and turned to pull her up the steps just as Carrie stepped out from the back. "Look who's here," she said to Carrie, but she narrowed her eyes in warning since Carrie wasn't smiling.

"Awesome," Carrie said, and Jen was relieved that she broke into a smile.

They settled into the deck chairs and started with the questions, as mothers do. "How's school? Any boyfriends? How's tennis season going?" Jen was a little disappointed when Bethany gave them pretty much one-word answers—until Carrie said she had to check on the ribs and disappeared into the back.

Suddenly, Faith, Jen and Maggy heard about the tennis season, her grades, how she felt about Rob and Cassidy—Jen was not a bit surprised that it was very little—and even what colleges she wanted to apply to.

But when Carrie came back and sat down beside

her, Bethany stared at her chips and guacamole. The rest of them tried to continue the conversation, but it was pretty apparent that Bethany didn't want to talk when Carrie was around.

The next time Carrie went to baste the ribs, Jen found herself alone with Bethany. Maggy and Faith had disappeared into the kitchen to start setting the table, and she turned toward the teenager. She'd always been one to call her boys out when there was something wrong, and she figured it couldn't hurt now.

"Okay. What's going on?"

Bethany mashed the guacamole around on her plate with a chip, but didn't raise her eyes.

"It's obvious that you don't want to talk to Carrie. She's very sad about it."

Bethany dropped her chip on her plate and let out a wry laugh. "Sure. Right."

"What do you mean? She loves you. She's your mother."

Bethany dropped her plate on the table and leaned back in her deck chair. She laced her fingers behind her head and looked out at the ocean. "If she loved me, I would have heard from her in the last four years, don't you think? She called for a while, but even that ended. She's gotten on with her life, and so have I."

Jen's heart quickened, but she knew getting angry

with Bethany wasn't the right way to go about this—if she could help it.

"That's not true. She thinks about you every day. Talks about you all the time. She's called you, sent emails every single week—you haven't responded."

"She has? I think I may have blocked her email a while back. I guess that's my point. She gave up, too. She could have tried something when she didn't hear back from me. She even missed my sixteenth birthday."

Now Jen's blood really was hot. Bethany had completely manufactured this story in her own head. Carrie had written every single weekend, without fail, and Jen knew that for a fact. She also knew some other things, and thought it was time that Bethany knew them, too.

"No, she didn't. None of us did. How did you like the 'Happy Sweet Sixteen, Bethany' sign covering the garage and all the balloons and streamers in the trees?"

"What? How did you know about that?"

Jen leaned back in her deck chair and folded her arms. "Because we did it. Faith, your mom and I took our lives in our hands to do that. Carrie even special-ordered the balloons with your name on them."

Bethany stared at Jen. "Cassidy said Armand did it."

Jen almost snorted, and covered her mouth with her hand. "Of course. But no, we did it. You wouldn't return any phone calls, and we didn't want to let the day go by without recognizing it."

"Oh," Bethany said quietly. "And she's emailed every single week?"

"Yep. It's hard for her, because you never respond, but she does it anyway. Wants you to know she loves you."

Bethany dug her phone out of her pocket and punched some buttons. Her eyes grew wide and she looked up at Jen.

"There are over two hundred emails from her in my spam file." She frowned, and swiped at her eyes with the back of her hand.

"Mh-hm. And when she thought you wanted to come and stay with her, she was ecstatic. Very excited, and hopeful that you two could start over."

"Oh," Bethany said, and she shoved her phone back in her pocket as Maggy and Faith came out the front door, giggling as they set food on the table.

Faith stopped and cocked her head, looking at Jen and Bethany. "Everything all right?"

Jen raised her eyebrows and looked at Bethany, who'd covered her face with her hands, her elbows resting on her knees.

Bethany rubbed her eyes for a minute, then dropped

her hands. She looked at Maggy and Faith and gave them a little smile.

"Yeah. Everything's fine. Anything I can do to help?"

Jen leaned forward and squeezed Bethany's knee. "Think about it, Bethany. She loves you. We all do. And we've missed you. You get to choose what this looks like now. It's your decision."

THIRTY-ONE

Carrie noticed that Bethany had been a little more talkative toward the end of the evening, but not a whole lot. She'd thanked Jen profusely, and she thought maybe she'd seen the sparkle of a tear when Bethany hugged her goodbye after thanking her for making all her favorites. She even handed them a plate of strawberry shortcake to take home with them.

"It sure was nice to see everybody," Bethany said when they'd gotten about halfway home. The boardwalk was mostly empty at this time of night, and the ocean was calm. The waves lapping at the shore were peaceful, and Carrie felt calm, too.

"They were all looking forward to seeing you. Thank you for coming."

Bethany nodded.

"What did Maggy say to get you to change your mind? I obviously couldn't do it."

Bethany took a quick glance at Carrie. "It wasn't anything she said. I just realized how long it'd been since I'd seen her, and Jen and Faith. I've known them as long as I can remember, and Maggy was the best babysitter ever. I guess I just realized I missed her."

Carrie was grateful for the darkness. She wouldn't have wanted Bethany to see the shock on her face.

"She missed you, too. We all did."

Bethany fell quiet and they finished the walk home in silence. As they turned the corner, Carrie noticed a box on the stoop, next to the front door.

"What's that?" Bethany asked.

"I hope it's what I ordered from Amazon," Carrie said, handing the leftovers to Bethany and reaching for the box.

She set it on the kitchen island when they'd gotten inside. She eagerly opened it, pulling out the big Keurig box, and the smaller boxes of coffee and tea.

"Yay. It came." She glanced at Bethany.

"You ordered a Keurig?" she asked quietly.

"I did. And this," she said, pulling out the box of green tea and organic honey. "The honey is from a special bee farm in Arizona. They make their honey only from the flowers of prickly pear cactuses. And I got some lemons today while you were out."

"That's my favorite," Bethany said, and she slowly stood, taking a step backward.

"I know. I asked Armand."

She glanced at Bethany, who had a strange look on her face that Carrie couldn't exactly read. When she didn't say anything, Carrie shrugged and began to set up the Keurig.

"I got some hot chocolate, too. Want some?"

Bethany hesitated for a moment, but said, "Sure. I'm going to run up to my room for a minute, though, if that's okay."

"No problem," Carrie said. "It'll take me a few minutes to figure this thing out, anyway."

Carrie stared after Bethany as she headed up the stairs. This was the most they'd spoken in the entire week since she'd arrived. She wasn't sure what changed, but she was glad for it.

She set up the machine and filled it with water. The two mugs she'd picked out were special—Bethany had made them for her for Mother's Day when she was in grade school, before the disaster.

Bethany hadn't come back down yet, so she quickly dialed Jen.

"What did you do?" she asked, lowering her voice.

"I just told her some hard truths, that's all. Is she talking more?"

"A little bit. I wouldn't say she's a chatty Patty, but I offered to make her some hot chocolate and she said yes. That's something."

Jen fell quiet on the phone for a moment. "Carrie, when she comes back down, be prepared for anything. And just be honest. Speak from your heart, and tell her the truth."

"Um, okay. What am I supposed to say?"

"Trust me. You'll know," Jen said. "I love you, and good luck."

In Carrie's experience, when someone wished her good luck it wasn't a huge vote of confidence. But she took Jen's words to heart, and squirted some whipped cream from the can she'd bought into Bethany's hot chocolate. And waited.

She finally sat down in the living room and started to flip through a magazine, her hot chocolate long gone. The whipped cream in Bethany's had melted by the time she heard footsteps on the stairs.

"Oh, hi. I thought maybe you'd fallen asleep," Carrie said as she pushed herself out of her chair. "Want me to heat up your hot chocolate?"

"Sure, thanks."

Bethany slid onto one of the stools at the kitchen

island as Carrie popped the hot chocolate in the microwave. When it was finished, she sprayed another dollop of whipped cream on top and slid it and a spoon toward Bethany.

"I remember this mug. Gosh, these don't even look like hearts. How old was I when I decorated this?"

Carrie smiled. "I think probably only six or seven. And they look like hearts to me."

"Well, that's what they were supposed to be. I remember," Bethany said. She took a sip of her hot chocolate and Carrie handed her a napkin when she ended up with a white mustache of whipped cream.

They both giggled, and Bethany said, "Thanks."

Carrie wasn't quite sure what to say next, but Bethany seemed to have something on her mind.

"You okay?" she finally asked when Bethany was almost finished with her hot chocolate.

"Yeah. Sorry I took so long upstairs. I had over two hundred emails that I had to read." She glanced up at Carrie beneath her lashes, and looked a little shy.

Carrie wasn't quite sure what she was talking about.

"Wow. That's a lot. Who were they from?" She reached up for a bag of popcorn and set it in the microwave.

"You," Bethany said softly.

Carrie frowned, confused. "You re-read all my emails? Four years' worth?"

"I didn't re-read them, no. I read them for the first time."

Carrie blinked hard. The popcorn began to pop, and all she could think of was that Bethany hadn't known she'd written her every Sunday. For years.

"You didn't read them before?"

Bethany stared into her empty mug. "No. I'm really sorry. I guess I was mad when—well, when everything happened and you didn't want me and made me stay at Dad's. I guess I marked them as spam, and they never came into my inbox after that."

"Whoa, hold up a minute. What do you mean I didn't want you and made you stay at your dad's house?"

"You know, when I stayed at his house instead of going back and forth. You didn't want me."

Carries heart stopped beating for a moment, and her throat seemed to close. Rob had assured her that Bethany knew why they were changing the arrangement —in her best interest. How could this have happened? She took a deep breath and realized exactly how it happened. Rob had lied. Again.

THIRTY-TWO

Jen's words popped into her head again—keep your heart open and tell the truth. So she figured she had to. She didn't want to cause problems between Bethany and her father, but she couldn't let her continue thinking that she hadn't wanted her.

She took a deep breath and asked for some universal guidance or divine intervention or something. She felt like she was going to need it.

She reached on top of the refrigerator and pulled down the big, pink box. She ran her hand over it and set it on the island, sitting down beside Bethany.

She took another deep breath and turned toward her daughter.

"Do you remember when you were going back and

forth every week? And every Sunday night you would get sick and throw up?"

"Yeah," Bethany said. "It was kind of hard."

Carrie nodded. "Right. And every Sunday, you kept getting sick, then started not eating at all."

Bethany nodded. "Yeah. I don't really know what that was about. It went away."

Carrie took a deep breath rested her hand on her heart, grateful that it had turned out the way she'd hoped.

"Good. And that was why we changed the arrangement. I'd talked to a counselor about it, and she said that it was too stressful for you. That you were having trouble with it, and we should choose a house as primary residence."

Bethany leaned back and crossed her arms, her jaw tight. "So you just gave me to Dad. And Cassidy. I didn't even know them. It had mostly been just you and me."

Carrie shook her head. "No, I didn't. I wanted you to stay with me. I asked your dad to agree to that. You'd be stable, we'd be together, and we lived right by school. He was busy with Cassidy and the restaurant, anyway, and I thought it was a no-brainer."

"Hm," Bethany said, her shoulders softening a bit as she leaned forward on the counter.

"I was shocked when he said no. That he wanted full

custody, and that I could have every other weekend and summers. I was waiting until you turned twelve to file the formal adoption papers, but you hadn't yet. So I had no rights at all since I wasn't your birth mother."

Bethany spun her spoon on the counter, without looking up.

"So how come that's not what happened? Why didn't that continue?"

"I was all set to take you every other weekend, but your dad and Cassidy had just started the reality show. It seems they were filming every weekend I was supposed to have you. I'm not sure I believed him, but I couldn't prove it. By that time, you were a little caught up in all of it and didn't want to come anyway."

"I guess I was, in the beginning. I don't know how I could have been so stupid. What a joke all that is."

"Well, at the time it was probably pretty exciting. But later, it was too late and you didn't return my phone calls. Or emails. But I see now, why."

Bethany stood and paced the kitchen floor for a moment, her hands in her pockets.

Carrie couldn't quite read her face, but it looked like a combination of anger, sadness and confusion. Which would be exactly what she was feeling, herself.

She stopped herself before telling Bethany that she'd cried herself to sleep for at least six months before the grief lightened. No sixteen-year-old needed to hear that. Even what she had heard so far was probably too much, but there was no way out of it now.

"What's in the box?" Bethany asked as her pacing slowed.

"I just wanted to show you that I hadn't given up on you. And I hadn't forgotten, either."

She took off the top of the box, and laid all of the newspaper articles on the island. The photos of Bethany, the articles about Bethany.

And her heart lifted as Bethany laughed when she finally laid out all of her school report cards, all the way back to kindergarten. And the book that she'd written for her on Mother's Day when she was four.

"Oh, my gosh, did I draw that?" she asked, pointing to a picture of stick figures, one taller than the other, both with dresses on. Or triangles, more accurately. The taller one's dress was orange with flowers on it, and labeled 'Mommy.' The other stick figure was labeled 'Me'.

"Yep. You did."

"I guess you wore crazy clothes even back then," Bethany said with a laugh.

"What do you mean?" Carrie asked, looking down at her bright, paisley orange bathrobe.

"Never mind," Bethany said.

Bethany took a few minutes to go through the remaining contents of the box. Carrie made them both another cup of hot chocolate, hoping that Bethany might stay for a while.

They laughed about the artwork, the little book about dinosaurs that Bethany had written in sixth grade and the book about butterflies.

"I remember I wanted to work at Jurassic Park," she said with a laugh.

"You did. Except you wanted to be a dinosaur, not a scientist."

"What is this?" Bethany asked, lifting out a green hat with a feather on it. It was small, but she tried to put in on anyway, which made them both laugh.

"I can't believe you don't remember. We got that on your first trip to Disneyland. It's a Peter Pan hat. And you wanted to be Peter Pan for Halloween. And you made us call you Peter for almost a year."

Bethany rolled her eyes. "I don't believe you."

"I have pictures in there somewhere. But ask your dad. He was really annoyed."

Bethany looked up at Carrie and smiled. "I bet." She set everything back in the box and carefully placed the lid back on. "Do you mind if I take this in my room? I'd like to look at some of this later."

Carrie nodded. "Of course."

"Thanks." Bethany glanced at the microwave and took an exaggerated sniff. "Popcorn smells good. Want to have some and watch TV?"

Carrie blinked a few times, not sure she'd heard correctly. "You want to watch TV? With me?"

Bethany smiled sheepishly. "Yeah. I'd like that. Do you have Netflix?"

"Yes. What do you want to watch?"

Bethany poured the popcorn into the bowl that Carrie held out. "How about Gilmore Girls?"

Carrie laughed, her heart lifting. "Again? Sure," she said as they headed into the living room and made themselves comfortable.

THIRTY-THREE

The fashion show was only a week away, and time had sure flown. Many Scrabble games had been won and lost, and Carrie was up by one in the ongoing tally. They'd played so many times because Bethany said she needed to be ahead by the time Rob and Cassidy got back, and Carrie was doing her best not to let that happen.

"You ready?" she called up the stairs to Bethany.

They'd gotten together with Dirk and Abby a few times in the last couple of weeks, and they were meeting them for doubles tennis today.

Bethany bounded down the steps, her rackets slung over her shoulder.

"Okay, ready."

"Hey, we're going to Jen's for Sunday dinner, right?"

"Yep. As always. It's that or starve," Carrie replied, picking up her own rackets and backpack.

"What do you think about inviting Abby and Dirk? You think she'd mind? I really like them."

Carrie considered that for only a second, knowing that Jen wouldn't mind at all. She texted her to confirm, and said she could pick up anything from the grocery store if she needed more.

NOPE, I've got plenty. Just bring yourselves. See you later! Ooh-la-la!

JEN AND FAITH had been teasing her relentlessly about Dirk. She couldn't quite figure out why. They were just two friends having fun with their teenage daughters. But she did notice again how handsome he was as he ran around the court. They'd decided to play against the girls today, and it went pretty well—except they lost. But they did realize that they played well together, and she immediately said yes when he suggested they join an adult league.

By the time they got to Jen's, they were all starving. Jen had burgers laid out and raised her eyebrows and a spatula toward Carrie.

"Of course," she said, and reached for the burgers but Dirk beat her to it.

Michael, Amber, Maggy and Faith were there, and Carrie made the introductions before heading back to the barbecue. Dirk followed with the plate of burgers, and a bag of buns.

"How do you always get barbecue duty?" he asked, setting down the burgers.

Carrie waved the spatula. "Everybody knows that I can barely boil water, but my dad taught me to barbecue. It's the least I can do to help out."

They chatted as the burgers sizzled. Carrie reached in to flip one of the them and since she was laughing, her finger grazed against the upper rack. She pulled her hand back and dropped the spatula. "Ouch!"

Dirk caught the spatula and frowned, gently taking Carrie's hand. "You need some ice. Be right back."

He returned in a flash, carrying some ice in a small plastic bag. He rested it on Carrie's finger, and she knew her hand should have felt freezing with the ice but it didn't. It felt warm.

She looked up at Dirk to thank him, and his eyes were trained on her. He looked concerned, so she smiled at him. She didn't want him to worry.

"It doesn't hurt that bad. I'm fine," she said softly. "Thank you, though."

His eyes softened, and instead of letting go of her hand, he squeezed it, pulling her a little closer. When he leaned toward her and closed his eyes, her heart beat faster and she closed her eyes, too.

"Hey, you okay?" she heard. They both took a quick step away from each other, and she pulled her hand away.

"Just wanted to check on you. Dirk said you burned yourself," Bethany said.

"Yeah. We were worried. Looks like we didn't need to be," Abby said from behind her, and they both giggled and turned to head back to the party.

"Uh, we'd better get these burgers off. I think they're done," Dirk said quickly, and Carrie handed him the spatula.

He made quick work of getting them on the platter, and she couldn't get back to the party fast enough.

Apparently, Joe, Mrs. Russo and Mrs. Grover had arrived while Carrie and Dirk were out back and there was quite a lively conversation going on.

"There isn't anybody else. Everybody wants to enjoy the show. The best dresses won't even be in the show if we don't find a couple of small types. Well, smaller than us, anyway."

"What size are the dresses again?" Carrie asked as

her heartbeat came back to normal and Dirk smiled at her.

Mrs. Russo's eyes traveled to Bethany and Abby and she raised her eyebrows. "Exactly that size."

Bethany and Abby looked at each other and back to Mrs. Russo.

"What do you mean?" Bethany asked.

Mrs. Russo explained the fashion show at the village and as she finished, Mrs. Grover stepped out the door holding the black, sequined cocktail dress.

"Wow," Dirk said, and Joe said, "Nice," in agreement.

"Why don't you girls come inside and try a couple of things on? The show is called 'Bold, Not Old' and we'd love to have you in it. All generations would be so fun." Mrs. Russo looked at the girls hopefully.

"After we eat, okay?" Jen said, setting down a bowl full of baked beans and another of barbecued potato chips. A cut-up watermelon was already on the table.

It was quite a feast, and everybody chatted happily. When Jen served Nana's famous chocolate lava cake, the girls ran inside with Mrs. Russo.

Jen was serving coffee by the time the girls came out, giggling.

"So you in?" Dirk asked.

The girls looked at each other and nodded. "It'll be fun. There's no tennis that day and we'd like to help."

The two older generations sat on the deck, each savoring sweet Port dessert wine that Joe and Mrs. Russo had brought while the kids did the dishes.

"Ah, this is the life," Joe said, leaning back in his deck chair as the sun set and the breeze picked up.

Carrie reached in her bag for the sweater she'd brought. It was October now, and the evenings cooled off quickly. Dirk took it from her to help her put it on, and Jen mouthed, "Ooh-la-la" when their eyes met.

Carrie looked around at her friends, and as it grew dark she could see into the house. She smiled, watching the kids do the dishes, and a sense of peace washed over her. This was how she'd thought her life would be. And it wasn't until she remembered that Bethany would only be around for one more week that the feeling faded.

THIRTY-FOUR

Carrie looked around when they'd come in. The auditorium at the Back Bay Village was decorated with autumn-colored flowers—orange, yellow and white—and Carrie would have added a bit of lime green if she'd been in charge. Thank goodness she wasn't.

Everything was ready to go. Jen peeked out between the stage curtains just for a moment to see how big the crowd was—and it was big. The ladies from Back Bay Village—no, there were people from all over Newport, Carrie noticed—seemed to be enjoying their lunches, eager for the entertainment.

"Uh-oh. Is that your mother at the door?" Jen squinted against the bright sunlight coming through the main door and pointed.

Carrie looked and determined that yes, it was her

mother. She just stared in her direction for a little bit, wondering why she was one bit surprised that her mother ignored Carrie's request that she not come.

"You told her you didn't want her to come," Bethany said, peeking out from behind the stage curtain. "Why did she ignore you?"

"I guess that's the million-dollar question that will never be answered." Carrie stood watching, her hands on her hips. Her breath started to quicken, and heat pricked her cheeks. "She's always ignored me, and I've had about enough of it, I think."

She flung back the curtain, stage right, and marched down the auditorium steps. Her mother had taken off her coat, handing it to the coat check girl and was arranging the feather in her fascinator. She did look lovely in a vintage traveling dress, but Carrie didn't really care. She'd had good reason not to want her mother there, and she intended to stand up for herself.

Her mother gave her a strained smile when she approached, turning to wave at friends around the room and barely acknowledging Carrie.

"Mother, we talked about this. I told you I didn't want you to come."

"My dear, there's absolutely no good reason for you to not want me to be here. These are my friends, too, after all," she said, smiling and waving although Carrie couldn't see anyone waving back.

"Hello, Grandmother," Bethany said as she came up behind Carrie, standing shoulder to shoulder.

Mrs. Westland took a quick glance at Bethany and waved her hand dismissively. "I asked you not to call me that, dear. Lovely to see you." she said as she glanced about the room. She hadn't even looked at Bethany but for a second, and Carrie's eyes met Bethany. She looked sad—and Carrie saw herself in her daughter.

Suddenly Carrie felt all the sadness of being treated exactly that way by her mother wash away. She realized that she wasn't angry anymore—she just felt sorry for her. All the memories Carrie carried in her heart of time spent with Bethany were more important to her than anything. If her mother didn't feel the same way—well, too bad for her. Carrie wouldn't trade them for a million dollars.

"Darling, there's nothing wrong with me being here." She leaned closer and lowered her voice. "If I hadn't shown up, it would have been noticeable. You understand—my reputation."

Carrie felt a calm pass over her, and she nodded. "Enjoy the show," she finally said, looping her arm through Bethany's and turning back toward the stage.

"I'm so sorry she's like that," Bethany said as the climbed the steps of the stage.

"You know, I've decided I just don't care anymore. If she doesn't want to have a relationship with her daughter, that's on her. I guess you can't choose your mother."

Bethany stopped Carrie after they'd slipped behind the curtains. "I know most people can't, but I can. And I feel very lucky."

Tears threatened to spill when Carrie drew Bethany in for a hug. "Thanks for having my back," she whispered.

Bethany took a step back and smiled. "Everybody needs a wingman. I learned that from my mom."

Carrie smiled and couldn't believe what she'd just heard. It was a little bittersweet—giving up on your own mom but becoming one all over again at the same time.

"You okay?" Jen asked when they entered the dressing room.

Carrie and Bethany shared a quick smile.

"Perfect," Carrie said. "Let's get this show on the road."

THIRTY-FIVE

They'd made all the final preparations when the only model who'd been missing confirmed that they wouldn't just be late—they couldn't come at all. They had four outfits just sitting there and there wasn't anybody in the show who was that size. The dresses were right between Bethany and Abby and Carrie and Jen. Nobody would be able to wear them.

All eyes turned to Mrs. Grover, who'd been helping backstage but had continued to insist she wouldn't be in the show.

Mrs. Grover glanced at the clothes hanging up that had no one to wear them. "Oh, no, I couldn't do it. Those are too racy for me."

"That's not even racy. That's practically what I wear every day," Mrs. Russo said with a roll of her eyes.

"Come on, Caroline, we need you. You're the only one that size."

Mrs. Grover fiddled with the top button of her cardigan and looked extremely uncomfortable. "Oh, no, I don't think I could. It's fun to watch you all do it, but it's not for me."

Jen watched as Carrie grabbed Mrs. Grover's hand and pulled her out a side door, onto the deck overlooking the back bay.

"What's that about?" Faith asked as she adjusted the peplum on the suit she was wearing from the 1950s. She adjusted the hat with a feather in it and glanced in the mirror.

Mrs. Russo glanced at the door. "We need Mrs. Grover to model. Hopefully she's trying to talk her into it."

"Oh, I wish she would. It's so much fun to dress up like this," Faith said with one last tweak of her feather.

"You look like Lauren Bacall in North by Northwest," Jen said. "This really is fun."

"And you look like—"

"Don't say Audrey Hepburn," Jen said with a laugh as she tied Nana's Hermes scarf over her hair and pushed on the big, dark sunglasses, finished off with some bright red lipstick.

"Exactly," Mrs. Russo said. "She really does."

They all turned when the door opened, and Carrie scooted Mrs. Grover back into the room. She nodded at the older woman, looping her arm through Mrs. Grover's.

"Okay. I'll do it."

Mrs. Russo clapped. "Okay, chop chop. We don't have much time, and you're going to have four changes of clothes. Come on. I'll help you." She grabbed Mrs. Russo's hand and pulled her back to the dressing area. Mrs. Grover's eyes were full of panic as she turned back and looked at Carrie, who gave her two thumbs up and a wink.

Jen laughed so hard she had to hold her stomach. "What did you say?"

"I told her that you only live once, and it's a lot more fun when you step out on the ledge."

"Hm. Guess she bought it."

"Had to think of something. It's good for her. She's really sweet, she just hasn't done much that's challenged her. It's never too late to start."

"Here, here," Faith said. "Don't I know it."

They all laughed, and the coordinator came through, shooing them all back and lining them up in order. They'd practiced the day before, and they all knew the route they were supposed to take between the big round tables, where they were supposed to turn, and where they were supposed to change into their next outfit.

Carrie was surprised that she was a little nervous, and Bethany caught her eye and smiled. Bethany and Abby were next to each other as they'd thought it would be fun to go from youngest to oldest.

Abby peeked out into the audience. "Oh, no. My dad's out there standing in the back. He's probably going to take video. Sorry, guys."

Bethany shrugged her shoulders. "My dad isn't even in the country. It's nice—we can watch the video later at the barbecue."

"I guess so," Abby said, and they straightened their vintage skirts, ready for their performance.

Carrie thought it was sweet that Dirk was "that" kind of dad, and she wished that Bethany had one of those. But she didn't, and they were all doing the best they could.

The music started and the announcer began, Carrie turned to Mrs. Grover behind her. "Just follow behind me. And walk in the same places I walk."

Carrie thought maybe they were all going to survive this. Mrs. Grover's face was pale, but she nodded. She looked cute in black capris, a turquoise top and and black-and-white checked hat.

Carrie did her best to show off the clothes, and when

she got to the back of the room and turned around, Mrs. Grover was just beginning to walk through the room. She looked as if she was going to faint, and Carrie thought she might have to catch her. As they passed each other, she gave the woman the biggest smile she could muster. Mrs. Grover tried to smile back but it looked like more of a grimace.

On their fourth round, Carrie's eyes grew wide as saucers. Mrs. Grover walked down the steps of the auditorium with an entirely different spring in her step. Her last outfit was gorgeous, and Carrie laughed out loud as Mrs. Grover spun several times, her hips in a brand new rhythm as she walked.

"You were great, Mrs. Grover," Carrie told her, and when they entered the dressing room arm in arm, everybody clapped and whistled.

Mrs. Grover blushed a little bit, but curtsied anyway.

"That was so fun," Jen said. "It'll be a hoot to watch the video back at the house."

They went out into the audience and answered questions for a little bit, and cruised by the table where the vintage jewelry was displayed for the silent auction. "Wow, those are some pretty big numbers," Dirk whispered to Carrie. "By the way, you looked great."

It was Carrie's turn to blush, and she was grateful

that nobody saw her. Well, she thought nobody had seen her until she caught Jen's eye, knowing what she was thinking.

"Come on, Caroline. Let's get out of these clothes. We need to go soon."

Mrs. Grover glanced in the mirror and smiled at her snazzy black satin cigarette pants, red sandals and black and red floral top from the 60s. She fingered the beads around her neck and turned to Mrs. Russo, her eyes shining.

"I think I'll just buy this outfit. And wear it to the celebration. What do you think?"

They all laughed, and Dirk was the first to say, "Great idea. You look fabulous," he said, and he winked at Carrie as he held out his arm for the older woman. She blushed as she took his arm, and the spring in her step was still there on her way to the restaurant where they would celebrate.

THIRTY-SIX

Carrie was up early the next day. She wasn't even sure if she'd actually slept. If she had, the anxiety of Rob picking up Bethany the next morning had made it fitful, at best.

She popped a coffee in the Keurig for herself and set up a cup with honey and lemon, just the way Bethany liked it for her tea. She wasn't sure when she'd get up—it was still a few hours before Rob would arrive—but Carrie couldn't help but hope it would be soon.

The month had flown by entirely too fast. They'd gone through so much together, learned so much—how could it be over? There was so much more to do. So many more Scrabble games to be played. So much TV to watch. So many tennis matches to win.

Her phone buzzed, the text ring tone startling her out of her worry.

YOU OKAY?

LEAVE it to Jen to worry about her. She hadn't had a chance to reply before another one popped up on her screen.

YOU DOING ALL RIGHT? Thinking of you.

FAITH HAD CHECKED IN, too, and Carrie wasn't surprised at that, either. Her heart swelled, knowing her friends were with her, at least in spirit. Her phone buzzed again, and she shook her head.

I HOPE today is awesome for you. I'm pretty sure it will be.

AS USUAL, Dirk was way more optimistic than she

was. She couldn't imagine how it could turn out awesome with Bethany leaving. To her mind, it was going to be the worst day of her life.

She'd barely set her phone down when it dinged again.

SENDING YOU LOTS OF LOVE, sweetheart. I hope you're doing all right.

SHE DIDN'T EVEN KNOW Mrs. Grover knew how to text, and it hit her square in her heart. It was almost as if Mrs. Grover cared about her more than her own mother did. Well, not almost. She did.

A rustling sound came from upstairs, and Carrie's stomach lurched. She knew Bethany would be coming downstairs soon, and she quickly wiped away a tear. She slipped her phone into her pocket, wanting to keep all that love and good wishes close at hand.

Thump, thump, thump. Bethany's suitcases bounced on each stair as she came down, her hair still wet from her shower and her tennis rackets slung over her shoulder.

Carrie felt frozen in place, and it wasn't until Bethany smiled that she thought she could talk.

"Ready for tea?" she asked, turning away and swiping the back of her hand across her cheek.

"Yeah, thanks. Who said you couldn't even boil water? I take umbrage at that statement on your behalf."

Carrie let out a sigh and laughed, her shoulders relaxing. "The coffee maker does it, but thanks for the vote of confidence."

"Every woman needs a good wingman, right?" Bethany said as she set her suitcases and rackets by the front door.

"Right," Carrie said, her hand tightening around the phone in her pocket. Everybody did need a good wingman, and she had several.

Bethany sat at the kitchen island and smiled when Carrie handed her her favorite mug, the one with the hearts on it. She squeezed the lemon as she looked around the room. "Thanks for letting me stay."

Carrie looked around at the pictures they'd framed and hung, her heart a little heavy. "It looks much better now. Thanks for the help with the decorating."

"You're welcome."

Carrie finished her coffee and set her mug in the sink. "Nope, right in the dishwasher. You can't get away with that if I can't," Bethany said, and they both laughed.

"Right. Want to play a game of Scrabble before your dad gets here? One last one for the road?"

"I can't. I got a text from Dad that said he'd be early. He should be here any minute."

Their eyes met and Bethany held Carrie's gaze for a long moment. "I'm sorry. I would have liked to play."

"Sure. Another time."

"About that..." Bethany began. She set her phone down on the counter and looked down at the marble counter. She picked at one of her fingernails a bit before she looked up, her crystal blue eyes soft. "I was wondering if maybe...well, if you thought it would be okay...oh, jeez. I don't know. Do you think maybe I could come back sometime? I mean, like, more often? This went really well. And I had a lot of fun. And I learned a lot. And...and I'm going to miss you."

Carrie did her best not to cry. At the beginning, they'd gotten off on the wrong foot and she never, ever imagined in her wildest dreams that this is what Bethany might want. Her heart felt like it was going to burst.

"I would love that. I can't think of anything I'd love more, to be honest."

Bethany crossed the kitchen to wrap her arms around Carrie, and when they separated, Bethany gently wiped a tear from Carrie's cheek. "Don't cry. It's all good. We get to start over."

Carrie noticed that a tear trickled down Bethany's

cheek, too, and she wiped it away with a smile. "Thank you. I appreciate you giving me another chance."

Bethany gave her another quick hug and smiled. "I could say the same to you. I wasn't exactly sweetness and light. I'm sorry about that."

"You were fine. Awesome. The best daughter anybody could ever hope for," Carrie said. "Even though I wanted to poke you in the eye a time or two."

They both turned toward the door as a horn honked on the street.

"I wouldn't have blamed you. You want me to invite them in?"

Carrie didn't have to think about that for more than a nanosecond. "Uh, no. I'll wave, thanks. Oh, here's a bag of Nana's muffins and some avocados for you to take. Jen sent them."

"Aw, thank her for me."

"I will."

Bethany opened the door and scooted her suitcases out. Armand hopped up the steps to take her bags and nodded at Carrie. Bethany grabbed her tennis rackets, and then turned back. "Can I see your phone for a second?"

Carrie handed it over, wondering what that was about. Bethany punched in some things, smiled and handed it back. "See that app right there? It's a Scrabble app. We can play together, take turns. We can keep in touch more that way. No cheating, though."

Carrie held the phone to her heart and followed Bethany outside. One of the dark windows of the limo opened slowly, and Rob nodded from inside. Carrie returned the nod, but smiled and waved at Bethany after Armand loaded the suitcases in the trunk of the limo.

Bethany stopped for a moment, smiled and waved. "And tell your friends everything's okay."

Carrie's eyes grew wide and she glanced at her phone, the texts from earlier front and center. She shook her head and walked down to the sidewalk. She watched the limo until it turned onto Newport Boulevard, heading back up to the mansion on the bay.

She took a deep sigh. She wondered how she'd gone so long not even aware that her heart had been broken. And she smiled at the thought that maybe now, it might again become whole. She and her daughter were definitely on the right track.

The limousine had barely turned the corner before Carrie's phone dinged with a text from Bethany.

"I forgot to say I'd love it if you'd come to my tournament next weekend. Bring Dirk. And look on top of the fridge."

Carrie frowned and turned toward the refrigerator.

On top of the box with Bethany's stuff was a pretty package with a bow.

She set it on the counter and stared at it a moment before she reached for the orange, satin ribbon and pulled the end of it.

She carefully removed the tape and slid off the wrapping paper that was covered with orange flowers.

Her breath caught when she pulled out the gift. Tears spilled before she even got to the mantle, where she gently set the framed drawing, her finger gently running over the words, "Mommy," and, "Me."

She walked over to the balcony and opened the slider, taking a deep breath of cool, salty air. Gazing out past the beach, the waves and to the horizon, she finally felt like anything was possible.

EPILOGUE

The crisp, fall breeze whipped Carrie's hair as she headed to Dirk's house to pick him up. Abby and Bethany's schools had a tournament against each other and they'd agreed to go together after Bethany had invited her.

He was waiting on the sidewalk when she pulled up in her convertible.

"Nice ride," he said. "I'd have one myself if I didn't have to cart clients around in that SUV."

"It's fun," she said, speeding off toward Newport Bay High School.

They found the bleachers and took their seats, falling into the rhythm of the hush that fell over the crowd when a ball was in play. It brought back memories of high school for her, and Dirk mentioned that he'd played in school, too.

"No wonder you're so good," she said.

They followed along as Bethany's doubles team beat Abby's, and Carrie smiled when they met at the net and shook hands, but Bethany hugged Abby. She looked over at Dirk and he was smiling, too.

"Thanks for all of your optimism before, when I wasn't sure how all this was going to turn out."

He nodded and smiled. "You're welcome. You know, Abby and I have had our share of issues, and she and her mother have had way more. Mothers and daughters—I don't think it's ever simple, even in the most uneventful of relationships. You guys had a lot more to contend with, in my opinion."

"We really did," Carrie responded, taking a quick look around to see if Rob or Cassidy were anywhere in the stadium. She wasn't one bit surprised to see they weren't.

"Great match, ladies," Dirk said when the girls met them at the side of the bleachers.

Abby smiled at Bethany. "Yeah, great playing, Bethany."

"And you, Abby," Bethany replied, and they fist-bumped with a giggle.

"How about some ice cream?" Dirk asked.

"Coach says I'm free to go if Abby is." Bethany looked at Abby hopefully.

"I can go, too. Hey, why don't we go down to the Fun Zone. Have a frozen banana?"

"Those are my favorite, too," Carrie said, and they jumped in the convertible, pulled on their visors and headed down Newport Boulevard. Carrie glanced in the back seat, not able to keep up with the giggles.

As she turned her eyes to the road ahead, with the beach on her right and the harbor on her left, she shook her head. Dirk was right. You never really knew how things were going to turn out, and she'd never in a million years expected to be this happy.

I hope you enjoyed Newport Beginnings!
Find out what happens when Faith tries to hold down two jobs—neither of them very well, and Carrie and Jen come to the rescue:

A Newport Sunrise

Have you read As Deep As The Ocean yet?

If you'd like to receive an email when my next book releases, please join my mailing list.

Printed in the USA
CPSIA information can be obtained
at www.ICGtesting.com
LVHW050032280724
786707LV00021B/268